Levels

ERIC WAL[illegible]

An elementary scho[illegible] Board of Education near Toro[illegible] started writing to entice his students [illegible] more creative, and each year he writes a no[illegible] for his class. Co-author of the Improve Your Child's Spelling series, he has written many articles for newspapers. Eric is also a social worker and family therapist who does crisis work at a community hospital.

When he is not spending time with his wife and three children, teaching, writing, or helping others, Eric plays basketball, makes up for lost sleep, and eats in first-class restaurants with drive-through service.

Stand Your Ground

ERIC WALTERS

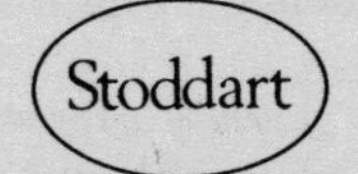

A GEMINI BOOK

Published in 1994 by
Stoddart Publishing Co. Limited
34 Lesmill Road
Toronto, Canada
M3B 2T6
(416) 445-3333

Third printing February 1996

Canadian Cataloguing in Publication Data

Walters, Eric, 1957–
Stand your ground

"Gemini young adult."
ISBN 0-7736-7421-7

I. Title.

PS8S95.A57S73 1994 jC813'.54 C94-931249-5
PZ7.W35St 1994

Cover Illustration: Albert Slark
Typesetting: Tony Gordon Ltd.

Printed and bound in the United States of America

Stoddart Publishing gratefully acknowledges the support of the Canada Council, Ontario Ministry of Culture, Tourism, and Recreation, Ontario Arts Council, and Ontario Publishing Centre in the development of writing and publishing in Canada.

Acknowledgements

I would like to thank Elsha Leventis for all her guidance, support, and encouragement in helping to make my dream of becoming an author a reality. And special thanks to my wife, Anita, and our children, Christina, Nicholas, and Julia, for having already made all my other dreams come true.

One

As the car moved slowly through the softly falling snow, I could feel my heart beating in time to the rhythm of the wipers. It was pounding against my chest so loudly that I was sure my father could hear it from where he sat beside me at the steering wheel.

The houses were all set well back from the street and looked neat and tidy and tiny. Each was brightly lit with strings of Christmas lights. Between the glare from these bulbs and the streetlights and the reflection from the snow, it was almost as bright as day. I would have welcomed darkness.

My father pulled the car over to the curb and stopped.

"It's just down there, the white house with the red pickup in the driveway," my father said. "Do you see it, Jonnie?"

I nodded.

"Well, this is it. You better get going," he continued.

I put my hand on the door handle and then hesitated. "Dad, I . . . I don't want to go."

"Want has nothing to do with it. Neither of us has any choice. You've got to go," he said with a hint of annoyance.

"I know, I know." I continued to stare out the front window, not wanting to make eye contact.

My father had told me there was more heat than ever before and that he had to travel hard and fast. So hard and fast that he needed to leave me behind. I wasn't sure who was after him this time. Probably not the police, because he wasn't afraid of them. And he was sure afraid now. We didn't talk about it, but I figured he'd got in over his head again with gamblers and didn't have the money to pay them.

"All you have to do is remember everything I told you. He might look as strong as a bull, but he's just about as smart as a streetcar. Just out-think him. I wouldn't leave you here if I didn't know you could handle him. Okay?"

"Okay. I know I can handle it," I answered.

"Good. I'll be back to get you as soon as I can. It won't take long. You'll be fine. After all, you're not a baby anymore, you're almost thirteen."

"Fourteen."

"What?"

"Fourteen. I'll be fourteen in January, remember?"

"Of course I remember. What kind of a father do you think I am? I just lost track. Half the time I don't even know how old I am, and right now I've got enough on my mind without you ragging me about something stupid like this. Anyway, now that you're nearly fourteen," he said sarcastically, "you should have no trouble at all. It's not like when you were a kid. Back then you were nothing but dead weight. Lately I've been thinking there might be hope for you."

I nodded. He was right. He was always right. I opened the door, grabbed my bag, and climbed out of the car into the cold night air.

"Bye, Dad. I'll see you later."

"Yeah, later. Take care of yourself, and remember

everything I've taught you. And, Jonnie . . . have a Merry Christmas."

"You, too." I stood there beside the car, feeling frozen to the spot.

"Don't worry, you'll do okay. Swallow hard and get going. You know I'll be back as soon as I can." His voice was calm and reassuring.

Silently I obeyed. The noise from the door closing was instantly captured by the snow and vanished. I walked away. I heard the soft purr of the engine as the car glided past me with its lights off. It quickly picked up speed and its tail lights glowed brightly as it came to a stop at the far end of the street. Big red rubies reflected in the snow. The headlights came on as it rounded the corner, and then the car disappeared from sight. He was gone and I was left here, alone.

I walked up the driveway and stopped behind the pickup. A layer of snow settled on my hat as I stood there gathering the courage to go forward. The tips of my ears and the ends of my fingers tingled in the cold. I wished I had some gloves. Maybe there was too much heat for my father, but it sure had left me out in the cold.

The lawn was bathed in the glow of the Christmas lights that hung from the eaves and clung to the two trees framing the walkway to the house. The path was guarded by a metal gate, which creaked loudly as I opened it. The snow crunched under my feet as I made my way along the walk, up the two steps, and across the wooden porch.

I took a deep breath. The air felt cold in my lungs. A shiver went through my whole body. I exhaled and watched my breath float away and disappear into the night sky. I wanted to follow it upward and away.

"You'll be okay, you'll be okay," I whispered to myself.

My arm felt heavy as I raised it and knocked on the door. I heard movement from within the house, then the porch light came on. The door opened and the doorway was filled with an immense man with grey hair.

"Good evening. Can I help you, young man?" he asked in a deep voice with a funny accent.

I took another deep breath. "I'm Jonathan."

"Well, hello, Jonathan. Now, what may I do for you on this very cold night?"

I paused and took one last breath. "I'm Jonathan . . . your grandson."

He bent down. His expression changed ever so slightly, and the friendliness that had been in his eyes faded away. As he moved closer, I felt his eyes burning holes right into me.

"Velta," he yelled over his shoulder, "you better come to the door. There is somebody here you will want to see."

* * *

That night I lay in the room they had given me. They'd told me that this used to be my mother's room. Now it was a sewing room and was filled with materials and patterns and a big cutting table. All of these things had been pushed to the side to accommodate a cot they'd brought up from the basement. The cot smelled musty, and it was a struggle to find a place to lie between the bumps and the lumps.

I thought about how my dad always insisted on going first class and how far this was from that standard.

The room overlooked the front of the house and

the street. That was important. I had to be able to see my father's signal when he came back to get me.

From the floor below I could hear them talking. I rolled out of the cot and crawled over to the heating grate on the floor. I could hear their words echoing up the ducts.

"Fruit doesn't fall far from the tree," he thundered.

"We are not talking about fruit," she answered firmly. "We are talking about a boy."

"Yes, he is a boy, but he is a boy raised by that man. I wouldn't let that man in my house, so why should I let his boy in my house?" he yelled.

"First, it is not your house, but *our* house. Second, he is not just that man's son, he is also our daughter's son and our grandson," she responded.

"How do we know he is our grandson? It has been over six years since we saw him." His voice was different now, not quite so angry sounding.

"Herbert, please, do not be silly. Of course he is our grandson. Could you not see our daughter's soft brown hair, the gentle features of her face? I could almost see her soul behind those clear blue eyes of his. Anyway, what harm could be done by offering him our home?"

"What harm? What harm? There is no telling what may come of this, but I would think it would not be good," he retorted. "Either way, I do not trust the father and I do not trust the son."

The voices became quieter and quieter until I couldn't make out the words. I just knew she was doing more of the talking. Finally the furnace came on, and I couldn't hear anything over the rumble and rush of the hot air. I sure hoped my first night wouldn't be my last. But I couldn't blame them for not wanting me. It had been a long time since I had seen them. A long time since the funeral.

One day my mother was alive and the next she wasn't. She was lying in a wooden box, holding a picture of me in her hands, surrounded by flowers. I was seven years old. Me and Mom had lived alone since I could remember.

My father used to visit sometimes, but he had stopped coming a couple of years before.

Most of what happened I can't even remember. Thinking back, it was like watching an old movie, with things all hazy and scratchy and dim, and I just couldn't follow what went on. Being there at the funeral was like being dropped in a deep well. I couldn't see or hear or even breathe. It felt like I wasn't really there, like it was a bad dream and when I woke up everything would be okay. She'd wake me up, make my breakfast, and we'd do things together. Everything would be okay.

It was never okay again.

The room was filled with people. A lot were crying. Strangers — everybody was a stranger — kept coming up to me, saying words, touching me, crying tears that fell onto my lap. Suffocating smells of sweat, cigarettes, alcohol, and too much perfume. To this day, those smells can still bring me back in my mind to that funeral home.

My mother's parents were there, one on each side of me. They were strangers, too. I'd never met them until just after my mother died. And I had never been to this town that had been my mother's home.

My grandfather was big, so big he seemed to me like a giant. His hands were massive, a thumb and two fingers on one hand, a thumb and three-and-a-half fingers on his other. I kept looking at his hands as he sat there folding and unfolding them on his lap. They were the only parts of him that were moving, almost like they were the only parts of him that were alive. Except for his hands, he looked like a carved stone sculpture on the side of a mountain. No tears flowed from his eyes. He looked angry, and I didn't know why. I sat beside him in fear, fear that he would turn those angry eyes toward me.

My grandmother ("just call me Oma") was all movement. She was little, and as we sat there, her head was almost level with mine. Her feet swung from the pew, just barely touching the ground. She shook, and her tears flowed like rivers. Everybody touched her and she touched everyone.

The service ended and I was led to a waiting car. We were going to put my mother into the ground. I looked out the back window to see a long line of cars and trucks flowing behind us, receding into the distance. Each vehicle had on its lights even though it was daytime. My mother always said that cars with their lights on made her think of diamonds. And the red tail lights looked like rubies. Diamonds and rubies.

The cemetery was on a small hill behind a church, overlooking the river and the town. I had never been in a cemetery before, never been behind the walls that always seem to surround them. I remembered a joke a kid at school had told me. "Do you know why they have fences around cemeteries? To keep people out 'cause they're dying to get in."

The procession drove through the gates and stopped. My grandmother held my hand as we walked over the grass toward the mound of dirt in the distance. As we got closer I could see the hole.

I didn't want to be there. Anywhere else, but not there. I didn't want to look at her being lowered into the ground. My grandmother let go of my hand, and

I slowly drifted back, through the crowd, until I found myself at the very edge of the circle of people.

I looked away and all I could see were row after row of headstones extending into the distance. Each one meant a person. I couldn't believe that that many people had ever died. Beyond the stone monuments, I caught a movement. It was a man, standing well away from the crowd, watching. I stared at him. He was at the edge of the cemetery, a car parked behind him, outside the gates.

With the preacher talking, the tears and sorrow blinding people, no one noticed one small boy moving slowly toward the solitary figure in the distance. When I got closer I knew it was him. My dad. It had been a long time since I had seen him, but I could tell by the way he stood there, by the fancy car parked behind him. I stopped walking and started to run.

As I reached him, somebody in the crowd must have noticed where I was going.

"I've come to get you, Jonnie. It's time to go," he said softly as he took my hand and we walked to his car.

We got in and he started the engine. Through the windows I could see the faces of the people as they surged toward the car. They didn't look sad anymore. Instead they looked angry and frightening. I didn't know why they were so angry, but I do remember being scared. I ducked down low and buried my face in my dad's lap as we drove away.

That day still haunts my dreams.

Two

For the first time in my life I was looking forward to going to school. School, come to think of it, anything, would beat having to spend any more time locked in with those two.

I think I'd been asked every possible question. She asked the questions and he just sat there, watching and listening. What did he think I was going to do, steal the silverware? As far as I could see they had nothing to worry about. There wasn't anything worth stealing. They didn't have a stereo, VCR, or even a TV.

Not a word was spoken between us as he drove me to school. The silence made me feel a bit nervous, but at least it was honest. What did we really have to say to each other? She kept pretending we were family. With him I knew where I stood. I didn't know him and he didn't know me. He didn't trust me and I didn't trust him.

He dropped me off in front of the school. She had already been in the day before and taken care of registration.

As I walked through the front door I saw their motto: "Together We Aspire, Together We Achieve." Cute. It sounded like something you'd see on a bumper sticker.

Vista Heights was like no school I had ever seen.

And, believe me, having been in twenty-four schools over the past six years, I was an expert.

It wasn't just that it was modern, but it was beautiful. The halls were wide and bright, skylights let sunshine in through the ceiling, murals and stripes in neon paints brightened the walls, carpeting covered the floors. If it wasn't for the kids shoving and pushing as they flooded the halls, you would almost think you were in a hotel. The Holiday Inn Public School. No question, this was going to be okay.

"Get out of our way, you stupid little townie!"

I pressed myself against the wall as seven or eight guys pushed past me. I watched them walk up the hall. As they moved along the corridor, other kids made space for them and yelled out greetings. They all had identical trendy haircuts and clothes, expensive sneakers, and that look of smug satisfaction. They were cool and knew it. Probably ordered me around because they figured they owned the school.

In every school there is always a group of kids who are the "in" crowd. You either made friends with them or kept out of their way. I didn't care either way. I wouldn't be here for either a long time or a good time.

The bell rang, and all the kids who had been milling around started to move. I asked directions to the office and then swam upstream against the crowd of people flowing to class.

When I arrived at the office, I felt a tap on my shoulder and turned around.

"Hi. You must be Jonathan. I'm Tommy. Mr. Roberts sent me down to get you. He said I should watch over you for the next few days. You know, make sure you don't get lost or anything. Come on, that was the ten-minute bell you heard a couple of minutes ago, so we only have a few minutes to get to class."

Without giving me a chance to answer, he turned and left the office, leaving me to scramble after him. I studied him out of the corner of my eye as I walked along beside him, dodging kids moving in the other direction.

He was dressed casually, a bit like a farmer, with blue jeans, work boots, and a plaid shirt. He was slightly taller than me, with a thin, muscular build. He walked confidently. Not a swagger, but like he knew where he was going and how to get there. Something about his face wasn't quite right. It looked like he had used his face to stop a barn door . . . more than once.

"How did you know who I was?" I asked.

"Mr. Roberts told me to get the new kid. In this town, everybody knows everybody, and I didn't know you. Have you met anybody else yet?"

I motioned toward the group of kids who had made my welcome so memorable. While everybody else was rushing to class, they were lounging around in the foyer, laughing and talking too loud.

"Well, I don't think you could say I met them, but that bunch of kids over there said something to me as I came in.

"Ah, so you've met the 'Royal Family' of Vista Heights. They probably weren't too polite to you either. Watch yourself around them. They run a lot of things and a lot of people around here. If you don't want trouble, don't cross them." With that said, Tommy changed course and walked straight toward the group.

Good, I thought, he's going to introduce me. But as we neared them, I saw their expressions change and realized that what was going to happen would not be good. I trailed helplessly behind him. The kids who were sitting down, stood up. Those that were standing, straightened up.

"How are you girls — I mean boys — doing today? Shouldn't you all be getting to class? If you don't know the way, I'd be more than willing to tell you where to go," Tommy snarled.

We brushed past them down the hall, and I could hear them cursing and yelling at us. I decided not to look back.

"I thought you said to avoid them or there could be trouble."

He chuckled. "No, no. I said if *you* don't want trouble, don't cross them. I never said I didn't want trouble."

Just my luck. New in the school and I've already got the "in" kids mad at me and the person they send to be my tour guide is a psycho.

* * *

The morning went by like a blur. There were all the usual introductions and instructions. Lots of names and rules, most of which I couldn't even hope to remember. I'm pretty good with names, but rules I've never really had to bother with.

My new teacher, Mr. Roberts, spoke with a funny accent. I could tell right away that he ran a strict class. Almost before the final notes of the national anthem had faded away, he introduced me to the class. Standing up there in front of everybody, I noticed that four members of the Royal Family were sitting together at the back of the class. Mr. Roberts asked me a few questions about myself. I could hear soft whispers and then a chuckle from the quartet at the rear. Roberts, who was facing me, with his back to the class, suddenly spun around.

"All right, stand up," he ordered, and the four slowly

got to their feet. "Since you are having difficulties being polite, I will provide special instructions . . . after school. Now sit down and be quiet."

He turned back to me and for a second before his expression softened, I saw fire in his eyes. I knew those four would be quiet now. After school they probably wouldn't be so polite.

Later, while the others were doing their work, I studied the interaction between the students. I especially watched those four sitting together at the back of the class. It was clear they were the centre of all that happened. Most of the other kids tried to act like them, do things to make the select four happy. Tommy and at least two other kids weren't even in the game.

When lunch finally came, I followed the crowd to the cafeteria and planted myself at an empty table. Tommy and two other kids I'd noticed in class, Vern and Stan, sat down and opened up their lunches. They explained to me the facts of life at Vista Heights. They were the townies.

A townie was somebody who came from the older part of Streetsville. Everybody else lived in the Estates of Vista Heights, a subdivision built over the last ten years on the rolling farmland that had circled the old town. The homes were big, beautiful, and expensive. They looked down on Streetsville the same way their owners looked down on the people who lived in the town.

Being a townie meant not having the right clothes, or enough money, or a fancy car, or a big house.

Streetsville had been around a long time, and before the new subdivision was built, everybody in town went to the same school. It was small, old, and getting pretty run down.

With the new homes would come an influx of new

kids who needed a school. There wouldn't be space in the old one. Vista Heights went up with the first houses, and its classes swelled with each new wave of houses. It was as modern and beautiful as the houses that surrounded it, with a well-stocked library, big gym, auditorium, cafeteria, baseball diamonds, soccer pitch, high-tech audio-visual equipment, and the best of everything.

At first there was no real problem between the kids in town and the Heights kids. After all, they hardly ever even met — except at sports meets.

Vista had the best equipment, excellent facilities, and top-flight coaching, while Streetsville Public School had so few kids it could hardly field teams. It had ratty old equipment and uniforms, a small gym that doubled as the lunchroom, and a small, bumpy playground.

Each time the two schools met, Streetsville won. And each time Streetsville won, the more angry and frustrated the Vista students became. And the more frustrated and angry Vista got, the more Streetsville won.

It would have been bad enough losing to another big, rich school, but to lose to these townies was a complete insult. That's why the Vista kids hated the townies.

Two years ago, the school board decided to close Streetsville. For people like Tommy, Vern, and Stan, who had been at Streetsville since kindergarten, moving to Vista for Grade Eight was almost unthinkable.

Vista may have been perfect in theory, but I could see the reality was far from perfect. The school may be pretty, but it sure wasn't welcoming.

Three

Each night we sat down to dinner together. It was always a slow, drawn-out process. I think it took us almost as long to eat the food as it took for the farmer to grow it. What a waste of time. After this ordeal I had to help them clear the table and wash the dishes.

As my hands were soaking in the soapy water in the kitchen sink, I eyed the mountain of dishes that still needed to be washed.

"Have you ever thought of using plastic plates?" I asked him.

"Plastic plates? Why would we want to use such things?"

"Well, they don't have to be plastic. I'd settle for Styrofoam or paper. Plates we could use once and then toss away. No washing or drying needed." There was a pause. I could see him thinking it through. Hello paper plates, good-bye dishpan hands.

"It is an interesting idea, Jonathan," he said, "but we enjoy the dishes we use. They belonged to Oma's mother. They came with us when we came from Holland forty-five years ago. Besides, to use such plates as you would like would make the earth cry."

How could I possibly argue with a response I didn't even understand? The only thing I did gather was that the answer was no. It was time to try another angle. As my father would say, "If at first you don't succeed, try another way to get what you want."

"Well, have I got a deal for you," I began. "Instead of all of us standing around bumping into each other, how about if we take turns doing the dishes? If one of you does them this month, the other next month, then I'll do them the following month. Sounds good, doesn't it?"

By the time my turn rolled around I'd be long gone, or if worst came to worst, I'd figure out some other way to keep my hands out of hot water. I don't know what my father would think if he saw me doing dishes. I know he never did a dish in his life.

He let out a loud sigh. "We greatly appreciate your offer, Jonathan, but I think we will continue with our present arrangement. After all, doing them together like this can be very entertaining."

"What do you mean entertaining?" I asked.

"Well, Jonathan, doing the dishes with you is sort of like watching one of those salesmen at a carnival. Always trying to sell somebody something they do not want and do not need. Always with the deals. But, in this home, the deal is very simple. We fix our food together, we sit down and eat together, and then we clean up together."

His tone left no doubt that this issue was not open for further discussion. I'd hit a dead end — for now.

I sighed and then continued washing the dishes in silence. I didn't have anything else to say to either of them anyway.

As I finished washing each dish, I took it from the water and handed it to her. Then she'd dry it and hand it to him to put away.

As I started on the forks, knives, and spoons, he spoke again. "Washing dishes is just part of showing appreciation for the work that was done in making a meal. You should learn to show a little gratitude."

"What's that supposed to mean?" I snarled.

"Gratitude. A thank-you, a little appreciation is what is to be expected. I haven't heard you say thank-you one time since you came."

"I'd say thank-you if I got something to eat worth saying thank-you for," I muttered under my breath.

"And what's more, you had better start getting home straight from school. We will not hold supper again. These last three nights you have been late. Where have you been?" he demanded. I gave him no response, didn't even turn to face him. It was none of his business. After school I'd been going to the video arcade in town. The kids were older, mostly school dropouts, and there was potential for a little action.

"If you do not get home by supper you can go hungry. I am sure that living with that man you have gone hungry many times before."

"I never went hungry. My father took good care of me," I snapped.

"Ha! Good care! Like dropping you off half dressed on our doorstep, alone in the middle of winter. Why did he not have the courage to face me at my door? That is not how a father acts!" he bellowed.

Deep in the dishwater my fingers instinctively curled into fists. Then I pulled them out of the sink and turned around to face him. "At least his kid wants to be with him. If you were such a great father, how come my mother ran away and never came back?"

He didn't flinch, but I could see in his eyes that my words had stung him. He took a step toward me. She stepped forward even faster and stood between us, facing me.

Without warning she took my hands in hers, and I felt my fists tighten and then gradually open. She turned them over slowly, peering at them intently. It felt strange, but I didn't pull them away. I wondered if she was losing it right before my eyes. I'd heard about old people going a bit squirrelly.

"Jonathan," she said quietly, "do you know whose hands you have?"

How in God's name do you answer a question like that?

Without speaking, she loosened her hold on my right hand. Then she took his left hand and held it up right beside mine. His hand was huge, weathered, with thick hair extending down each finger to the knuckles. Half of his baby finger was gone. A simple gold wedding band was on the next finger.

"Bertje, look. He has your hands. Jonathan, you have your opa's hands!"

"Great," I thought to myself, "I have the hands of a man who doesn't have enough sense to hang on to his fingers."

But as I stared down at my hand and his, I could see she was right. My hand was a smaller, softer version of his.

"You know, Jonathan, your opa has magic in those hands. The things he can build and create! Another thing, a boy's hands are like a puppy dog's paws. A little puppy with big paws will someday be a big dog. Someday you will grow into your hands and you will be a big man, maybe even as big as your opa."

I pulled my hand away from her and turned back to the sink. I held my hands above the water for a second and thought about what she had said. Then I pushed them both deep into the still-warm, murky dishwater.

***

Dear Dad,

I know I'm only supposed to use our letter drop in an emergency, but this *is* an emergency. I don't know how long I can stand it here. This has been the longest two weeks of my life!

I can't believe these people. It's the 1990s but they act like it's the 1890s. Bad enough they've never been to McDonald's (I thought the old man was just kidding when he said, "What do you mean McDonald's? The old farmer with the animals everywhere?"), but they have the strangest ideas about eating.

First off, we all sit around this big table in the dining room. She insists that I scrub myself clean and dress for dinner. The table is set like we're expecting the Queen of England. Fancy placemats, cloth napkins with silver napkin rings, big and little plates and cups and saucers in this matching pattern with stupid little flowers, knives and spoons, and lots and lots of forks. I tried to talk them into using paper plates, but the old man wouldn't go for it. He won't go for anything.

Each meal starts with a prayer. Can you believe that? A prayer! I always pray that when I lift my head there'll be some decent food on the table, like a cheeseburger, fries, and a Coke, but so far this is one more prayer that's gone unanswered. Instead, we have course after course of the strangest foods you've ever heard of. We eat things with names like hopscotch and Draino and beetle brains and clapstuck. How could anything called clapstuck possibly not taste like slime?

The only hope would be if I could wash away the taste with something good to drink. No such luck. As if the food wasn't bad enough, there's nothing to drink but juice. Sometimes it's apple or orange juice, but it's just as likely to be pineapple or pear, raspberry or blueberry, or carrot or broccoli. This must be the only house in the whole world where you not only have to eat your vegetables but drink them as well.

The dinner plates are as big as hubcaps, and she piles on so much food I'm afraid the table might collapse. She wants me to eat everything because she thinks I look too thin. If I don't finish, she gets this look like she is either worried I must be sick and running a fever, or hurt because I don't like her food.

Throughout the meal, when I'm not forcing this stuff down my throat, I'm expected to make polite conversation. "What did you learn in school today?" "Tell us about your friends." "Would you like help with your homework?" "What do you want to be when you grow up?" It's like being interrogated by the Polite Police.

I really miss eating burgers while watching TV. The big problem here is that these people don't have a TV. Let me write that again, because it's hard to believe. THESE PEOPLE DON'T HAVE A TELEVISION!! I mean, like even the Flintstones had a television. Unbelievable.

I've had some fights with the old man. He's made all sorts of stupid rules that he thinks I'm going to follow. He wants me to come straight home from school. When he does let me go out, I have to be in by 9:00, in bed with the lights out by 10:00. Unbelievable.

Lucky for him there isn't anything much to do here, so I hang around the video arcade in town. I've taken the locals for a few bucks and set up a scam, but it's all small-time stuff. Since they're going to throw me in my cell at 9:00 every night, I'll make sure to watch for your signal. I can see your car from my bedroom window if you park where you let me off.

I don't know how much more of this I can take. Please, please, please, please, hurry up and get me. Please!!!

Jonnie (lost in space and time)

P.S. If you can't come right away, could you at least send me a large order of fries?

P.P.S. Hold the gravy. It would probably leak out of the envelope.

P.P.P.S. HURRY!

Four

"Hey, townie, come on over here. We need your help with something," bellowed Justin from across the school lobby.

He was installed in his usual place by the front doors, with Alexander right there beside him, surrounded by half a dozen of their friends. I held my breath and hoped that they weren't talking to me.

I'd learned enough in life to know that if there were two sides fighting each other, make sure you're on the winning side. Almost always the side with money wins. I wanted to get in with the Heights kids, but so far they kept pushing me aside. I was just a townie to them. I might be a lot of things, but a townie I wasn't. Maybe my grandparents had townie tattooed on their foreheads, but I was different.

Over these first couple of weeks of school I'd heard Justin and Alexander snickering at me, but I pretended that I either didn't hear them or didn't understand that their comments were directed at me. I looked away and kept moving. Maybe they weren't even talking to me.

"Hey, new townie, I'm talking to you! Come on over here now!" he yelled. "Don't make me send some of the guys over to get you." His voice was loud and angry.

I turned and walked across the lobby to where they

were sitting. My feet felt heavy and my chest felt tight. Justin's loud threat to me had slowed down the traffic flowing by. People had stopped talking and walking and now stood waiting to see what was going to happen next. I felt eyes staring at the back of my head as I walked forward. I stopped just in front of Justin. He was perched on a wall, and I had to look up to make eye contact. Sitting up there, surrounded by his entourage, he made me feel like I was before a king sitting on his throne.

"Good, good. Glad to see you're only a little deaf. Now listen, townie. Alexander and I are having a little disagreement and we need your help to solve it."

"Yeah," said Alexander with a big smile on his face, "you see I think you're more ugly than you are stupid."

"But," continued Justin, "I'm positive you're much more stupid than you are ugly."

My brain just locked up. I was caught between a rock and a hard place. If I didn't answer I'd be burned in front of half the school. If I tried to burn them back, that would be the end of whatever slim chance I might have of ever being part of their group. Worse still, they'd probably jump me, now or later, and beat the stuffing out of me. Either way I'd look like a fool. If I stayed quiet though, at least I'd be a fool whose face was still recognizable.

"You see, Alexander, I'm right. He's so stupid that he can't even talk," goaded Justin.

"Just look at him, standing there with that dorky look on his face. He sure is one ugly dude," responded Alexander.

I could hear giggling and chuckling. I didn't want to look around at the big crowd I could feel had gathered to watch me being baited. My dad would know how to talk his way out of this one.

From behind me came a voice.

"Actually he isn't half-bad-looking." It was Tommy. "It's just that, compared to you two, most of us aren't that good-looking."

The noise from the crowd stopped abruptly, like they'd been frozen. Everyone listened in silence.

"Matter of fact," he continued, "you two guys ain't just handsome, you're downright pretty. Pretty hair, pretty clothes, pretty shoes — such pretty boys. Don't you think so, Jonathan?"

I had no idea what was happening or where this was leading or how I was going to get out of it. I did know I felt a lot better having Tommy at my side. I nodded ever so slightly. I figured they wouldn't get any madder because I said they were good-looking.

"Why don't you shut up, Tommy," snarled Alexander.

"Yeah, butt out of it. This isn't your business," added Justin.

"What a shame two such pretty guys have such ugly mouths. When your mothers dressed you this morning, didn't they tell you to be polite little boys?" Tommy asked.

I could hear giggling behind us. I took a quick look around and noticed a few familiar faces. I had hoped to see either Vern or Stan, but they weren't anywhere to be seen. One face that did stand out belonged to Stacy. She was a girl in our class. She wasn't a townie either, but she was friendly and had talked to me in class.

Alexander and Justin got off the wall, and along with three of their friends, moved toward us until we were just a few feet apart. The others were studying the action with more interest than they'd probably shown in school all week. I wanted to back off, but the crowd squeezed in on all sides.

"Jonathan, can I ask you a question?" Tommy asked. It felt like I'd forgotten how to even talk. I nodded.

"When they were asking you that question and you were just standing there, not talking back, staring at them, what were you thinking about?"

There was now total silence. Every eye was on me. Every ear was craning for my answer. I was already in over my head. In the corner of my eye I saw Stacy standing there watching and listening. I wasn't sure how this would all end, but I knew it wouldn't be with me being their buddies. Maybe I'd have to put up with a little garbage for a couple of weeks until my dad got back.

"Well . . . ," I started hesitantly, "I was just picturing Alexander and Justin's mommies powdering and diapering them before sending them to school in their matching party clothes."

A roar of laughter erupted and then rushed in from all sides.

"That's it. Right now, we're going to do you guys in," roared Alexander.

"Don't worry, Jonathan," Tommy yelled. "They fight like they're still in diapers, too!"

Suddenly the ten-minute bell rang. I was so startled I jumped straight up into the air. At that same instant, Alexander rushed straight toward me. I stood there, too surprised to even raise my hands, as he caught me with a straight punch to my nose. The pain shot up like a rocket, between my eyes and into my skull. Blood poured out of my nose as my legs buckled and I slumped to the floor. Through the tears and the blood I saw Tommy smack Alexander on the side of the head, knocking him backward. Justin and two of the others grabbed Tommy and wrestled him down to the ground, pummelling him with their fists as he fell.

Through all the noise I heard a man yelling, "WHAT'S GOING ON HERE! WHAT'S GOING ON HERE! EVERYBODY OUT OF MY WAY!"

Tommy quickly got to his feet and grabbed me by my shirt collar, pulling me up. The teacher was having trouble getting through the crowd — by now, most of the school had gathered in the lobby — and he couldn't see what had been happening. Tommy moved me into the crowd while Justin and his pals blended into the surrounding mob.

As Alexander moved away, he yelled over his shoulder, "We took care of the new townie, but we'll settle with you later, Kraemer."

Tommy ignored the taunt and steered me into the nearest washroom. He grabbed a handful of paper towels from the dispenser and soaked them in cold water.

"Here, hold this tight. It'll stop the bleeding." He pressed the cold towels against my nose. "Does it hurt very much?"

"It hurts, but not as much as I thought it would," I answered as I slumped to the floor. The cool tiles felt good against my back.

"What do you mean, not as much as you thought it would? You never been popped in the nose before?" He sounded like he couldn't believe such a thing could be possible. Tommy sat down right beside me.

"Nope. First time I've ever been in a fight. I've always been able to talk my way out of these things before," I said.

"Talk your way out? It looked like you'd completely forgotten how to talk when I got there."

"I was just working out what I was going to say," I lied. I changed the subject. "What jerks, calling me a

›wnie. My father has more money and a fancier car ıan any of them."

"Jonathan, unless your grandparents moved up to ıe estates last night, you are a townie. As long as you ve in the town, that's what you are," Tommy said.

"But I don't live here. I'm just visiting. I'm no ›wnie," I answered, making townie sound like a disase, the way Justin always did.

Tommy shook his head slowly. "Maybe both those uys were right."

"What do you mean?"

"Well, sitting here with a big wad of paper towels uck to your face, you do look pretty ugly, and if you ıink being a townie is such a bad thing, then you must e pretty stupid."

He got up and offered me a hand. I accepted, and e pulled me to my feet. "Come on, we had better get › class. You got a lot of things you need to learn. Iaybe now at least you know you won't change the ay they see you."

I took the wad of wet towels from my nose. The leeding had stopped. I tossed it toward the garbage an in the corner, but it bounced off the rim and fell › the floor. We walked out of the washroom into the ow totally deserted lobby.

"You've never been in a fight in your life," Tommy epeated, more to himself than to me, shaking his ead as we hurried down the hall. "Maybe you're right. Iaybe you're not a townie. Kid your age who's never een in a fight before has got to be from another lanet."

Five

"VERN . . . WAIT UP!" I yelled.

He had already left the school yard as I ran out th front door of the building. He stopped and lean against a car, waiting as I trotted to catch up. My heav winter boots and book bag and the snow on th ground made running difficult, and it took away m breath.

He started to walk again the instant I reached hi side. Over the past few days I'd tried to become friend with Tommy, Vern, and Stan. They weren't my firs choice, but now they were my only choice. I'd need few people on my side if those guys went after me again

"You move pretty fast," I said as I moved beside him "You're always gone before I get a chance to talk t you."

"Yup."

The kids in the lower grades had a bus to take them home from school. The rest of the townies had a lon walk home. When school ended, Vern was always gon like he had been shot out of a gun. He was a big kid with square shoulders and blondish hair. He and Sta and Tommy were best friends. Unlike Stan, who wa constantly smiling or laughing, Vern appeared to tak everything very seriously. He seemed to be a goo tudent, but the thing he was best at was leaving the uilding at the end of the day.

"The way you leave so quickly after class, you must e glad to get out of school." I tried another angle.

"Nope."

"You need to get somewhere?" I asked.

"Nope."

"You just like walking fast?" I asked, hoping for nore than a one word answer.

"Nope."

I was struggling, not just to get more out of Vern, ut to catch my breath. I was doing half the walking nd all of the talking. "Why, then, do you take off so ast after school every day?"

Vern didn't answer. He just kept walking, and I tayed by his side. I was thinking of another possible uestion when he responded.

"I just like to get away from Vista . . . back down to he town."

"Yeah, I can understand that. I don't like it up here ither," I said, grateful he had finally spoken more han one word.

"You know, Jonathan, it's not so much that I don't ike it here, but it just doesn't feel right. Sort of like it sn't mine. Up here there's only . . . trouble for me," e said.

"What kind of trouble?" I asked, although I was retty sure what his answer was going to be.

"What kind? You looked in the mirror lately?" Vern sked.

I touched my nose with a gloved hand. It was still a ittle tender. I had told my grandparents I had bumped nto a door when they asked about it the night of the ight. She had gotten me a cold compress. He asked me the name of the door but didn't pursue it any farther. He was no fool.

"There's nothing but trouble up here for us. The kind you and Tommy got into. The type Tommy's always in," Vern continued.

I could understand what he was saying. I wish I could've stayed out of things.

As we got farther from the school, Vern slowed down our pace. I could feel he was more relaxed now. I figured I could get some more answers out of him.

"Vern, when Tommy and I were leaving, after the fight, Justin yelled something about settling with him."

"First off, Jonathan, it wasn't really a fight. You'd have had to throw a punch back for it to be a fight. What it was, was you getting smacked in the face. Second, why ask me? Why not ask Tommy?"

"I already tried. Twice. He wouldn't give me a straight answer, and I know you're always straight with people," I said. Maybe he'd take this as a compliment and give me the answer I needed.

"I figure it's just a matter of time till there's a fight. Townies against the Heights kids."

"A big fight?" I couldn't hide the shock in my voice, and my stomach got all queasy.

"Don't worry. Nobody expects you to go. Besides, they already showed the whole school that you aren't any threat, unless you include maybe bleeding on their nice clothes."

I decided I'd better ask another question fast. "How did it start?"

"In the beginning of the year mostly we just traded insults. As it got closer to Christmas, a couple of times it looked like it was going to come to blows, but a teacher always came along. Then they started talking about a big rumble up at the water tower. Problem is there's a lot more of them than there are us."

My stomach was all tied up in knots now. I'd spent the better part of my life avoiding fights, and it had worked pretty well, at least until I got here.

"You really think it's going to happen?" I asked nervously.

"Yeah, probably — sooner or later."

"Are you going to go?"

"Nope. It wouldn't be any different than the skirmishes at school. No matter how many of us show up, there'll be more of them. No way we can win. Of course, it doesn't matter to Tommy. He's too stubborn to even think about losing."

Vern's voice sounded different, almost far away, as he continued. "And besides, my pa told me not to get into any more of that stuff."

"I guess my grandfather wouldn't want me to get into fights either." It was as good an excuse as any to justify my staying away.

"Well, part of it is because he doesn't want me in fights, but that's not what he's afraid of. My pa runs his own landscaping business. You've seen our truck, haven't you? Four Seasons Landscaping. Most of his business is up on the hill, in the estates. He says he could lose customers if they find out his kid has been fighting with their children."

I nodded. In the short time I had known Vern, I had never heard him put more than four words together in a sentence. I knew this wasn't easy for him.

"My family does all right. But we depend on those people. Things weren't as good before they came. Pa says sometimes you gotta walk away. Sometimes a man just has to walk away from a fight."

Sometimes a man has to do more than walk, he has to run away fast, I thought. I had only one more question.

"Vern, if it comes to that, if there's going to be a fight up at the tower, who'll go up there with Tommy?"

He turned away and then answered so softly I could hardly hear him. "Nobody. Probably nobody."

"Nobody?" I echoed in surprise.

Vern heaved a big sigh, and a shudder seemed to run through his entire body. We walked along in silence. I saw his lower chin start to shake and I knew that Vern, good old solid, serious, solemn Vern, was on the verge of crying. Finally he spoke.

"I know what you're thinking, Jonathan. How can I let Tommy go up there by himself when he's my friend? What sort of a friend am I? How can I desert him?"

Vern had no idea what I was thinking. I was trying to figure out the best way to put even more distance between me and all of this. There was no way in the world I'd get any deeper into this mess than I already was.

Vern continued. "Anyway, Tommy says he likes it better by himself. He says that we'd just get in his way and if there's less of us there'll be less of them."

We kept walking. I didn't have anything more to say. I probably had asked too many questions already. I just wanted to get away from even talking about that water tower and fighting.

Vern stopped, grabbed my shoulder, and spun me around to face him.

"You know what's the stupidest part about fighting, Jonathan? The Heights kids are right. We don't belong. At least not up there at that school." His voice cracked over the last few words.

He turned and ran off so I couldn't see the tears.

Six

The second Saturday after school started, I half opened one eye to see my grandfather standing at the foot of my bed. He was wearing a pair of denim overalls and a silly-looking painter's hat.

"Wake up, Jonathan. It is time to get going."

"I'm not going anywhere," I mumbled into my pillow, "don't you know what day it is?"

"It is Saturday. We have much work to do, so the sooner we get going, the sooner we will be done," he continued. "You will sleep better at the end of our day's work."

"I'd rather sleep better at the start of the day," I answered as I pulled the covers over my head. "What time is it?"

"It is almost 6:30, and we have already wasted part of the day. Get up," he instructed.

"No way. There's no way I'm getting up. It's way too early." I yawned. "Anyway, don't you know about child-labour laws?"

I turned over and put the pillow over my head. I could feel him still standing there beside my cot. The short silence was interrupted.

"I think you better know about the child-labour laws in this house. If you do not labour, even if you are a child, you do not eat. Breakfast will be ready in two minutes for all those who will be working."

I heard the creaking of the hardwood floor as he retreated across my room and down the stairs. I'd show him he couldn't boss me around. Half a minute passed. A full minute. I started to think about the days with my father when I had gone hungry because there was no food in the house. Maybe it was best to get up, have a little breakfast, and at least check out what sort of work he had in mind.

I tossed off the covers, threw my legs over the side of the cot, and stood up. Or rather tried to. Three weeks on this fold-up cot had given me kinks and aches in places I didn't even know I had places. I pulled on a pair of jeans and a sweatshirt I had left in a pile beside the cot when I climbed into bed last night. As I moved through the hall and down the stairs, as always I closed my eyes and kept track of how many steps it was to the staircase and how many down to the kitchen. It was important that I know the layout of the house in case I needed to sneak out in the middle of the night.

My grandparents were sitting at the table. Both their plates were half empty. A third setting was at the table, a mountain of food piled high on the plate. These people ate big at every meal. I figured I'd eat breakfast and even if I decided not to help, I'd be set for the day. After all, what was he going to do, make me give back the food?

"Good morning, Jonathan," she sang out. "I know you probably slept not too good, but at least you can eat better."

She scrambled out of her seat, grabbed the frying pan, and loaded on another layer of eggs before I'd even put a fork to the mound that was on my plate.

"If you are to work like your opa, you had better eat like him, too."

"Yes," he added, "we will do a good day's work, so you better eat. Afterwards you will sleep better. Working hard is good for the soul. It helps to build character."

"Yeah, great, just what I need," I answered.

He ignored my shot completely.

I was curious, and more than a little bit anxious, about what he had in mind for me.

"So, what are we going to do?" I asked, trying to be casual as I fished for clues while shovelling down the food.

"We are going to finish up a little project I have been working on in my shop for the past week," he said. With that, he got up and took his plate and cutlery over to the sink. "Thank you for the good breakfast, Mama, but it is time to get moving. There will be no sleep for Jonathan tonight until this job is done."

He moved to the back door, took his coat off the rack, and slipped it on. I jumped up from the table and followed, now even more nervous than before. By the time I had put on my coat and got to the door, he was already striding across the yard toward the garage. As I hurried to catch up, I heard the door open behind me.

"Herbert," she hollered, "you make sure that he is all right. Herbert, you take good care of Jonathan. Do you hear?"

Without turning around, he waved his hand and answered, "Yes, Mama, do not worry. He will be fine. A little work will not kill him."

I felt even more nervous. I was at his side as he unlocked the door and then proceeded to turn on the overhead fluorescent lights. We walked in. I looked around.

This was my first time in the shop. I hadn't paid much attention to the building behind the house. I just figured it was some kind of garage. Now that I was inside I realized that it was a lot bigger than I had thought. While it could have easily held four or five cars, there was only the door that we had passed through. All of the space was filled by machines.

Some of them I recognized from shop class. There were circular saws and drills. Others, I had no idea about. Everything was shiny and clean. You could eat dinner off the floor.

"Come on now, Jonathan. We have work to do," he said.

I swallowed hard, trying not to sound scared. "That was silly of her to be worried about something happening to me in here. What could happen?" I wanted him to convince me that I had nothing to fear.

"You are right, Jonathan. There is nothing that will happen to you today, but things do happen." He held up both hands to show the places where fingers used to be. "Accidents do happen, but not today and not to you."

I stuffed both my hands deep into the pockets of my jeans.

"Come. I want to tell you all about what these machines do and what they can do if you do not respect them. Let us start with this one here."

We moved to a large circular saw. He threw on the power and fed in a piece of scrap wood. The steady noise of the engine was replaced by a high pitched howl as the teeth ate into the wood, throwing sawdust flying into the air. He turned off the machine and the sound echoed away.

"I call this one Jaws. Do you know why?" he asked.

I thought about how its teeth ate through the wood.

Then he held up his right hand to again show the missing parts.

"I could not get these two fingers back, but I always held on to the machine that ate them."

I felt a sudden rush to my stomach.

"Do you know why I always kept the machine that did that, Jonathan?"

Because you're a complete idiot, I thought to myself. I shook my head.

"For one reason, because it is a good machine that always worked well, and second, to always remind me to think before I do. I try not to make the same mistake twice. Unfortunately there always seem to be new mistakes to make."

I nodded because I knew that was the expected response.

"Let us continue on our tour then."

* * *

Over the next ten hours we didn't even come up for air. My grandmother came in with our lunch. I overheard her talking to him about "their order had arrived" and she went away giggling like a schoolgirl.

The time passed incredibly fast. He showed me how to stain some wooden posts he had made earlier. I even got to choose the colour we stained them. I picked a light honey finish. This pleased him. He said it complemented the grain and texture of the wood. I really didn't know what he meant, but as I held the piece of wood and ran my other hand over it, I just knew this was the right stain.

The very best part was watching him work with a machine called a lathe. He strapped on a big piece of wood that was almost two metres long and twenty centimetres thick. Spikes and clamps at both ends held it tight. It was sort of like those things you stick into the ends of corn on the cob to hold it while you eat. Then he started the machine, and the wood spun around and around at incredible speed.

I watched in fascination as he took a series of chisels, and resting against a support, pressed them into the spinning timber. When the chisel met the wood, there was a loud scream, and bits of sawdust were thrown off into the air. Some remained suspended in the air, while some landed on my clothes and caught in the back of my throat. His hair and clothes were covered, and he looked like he had just come in from a snowstorm.

There was a smell of burning wood in the air, a bit foul and yet sweet to the nose. Over the noise of the machine itself and the wood meeting the chisels, it was almost impossible to talk.

He motioned me over and helped me to press the chisel against the revolving wood. It was like a knife carving into a piece of very cold butter. It gave way slowly but steadily.

More amazing than what was being done, was what was being made. Out of that lump of wood came the shape of another post. A thick, graceful, curved surface, topped by a large ball. I remember once reading about a sculptor who said he just helped the shape inside the rock come out. It seemed like the same thing with the wood. My grandfather was an artist freeing this post from inside the timber.

Finally satisfied with his work, he stopped the machine and unhooked the almost finished product.

"Did you like that?" he asked.

"Yeah, it was fun," I answered.

"You did well. You have a good feel for the wood.

But, maybe I should have told you . . ." He let the sentence trail off into silence.

"Told me what?"

He held up his left hand this time. "I lost the finger of this hand on a machine like that one, only bigger. You work too fast, not being careful, hit a knot, and pop." He clapped his hands together. "No more finger." He wiggled the remaining fingers on both hands. "It is a sound you do not soon forget."

A shudder ran through my entire body. He noticed and chuckled.

"It is not so bad, Jonathan. Believe me, if you ever have a choice between a quick pop with a lathe or a quick cut with a saw, choose the pop."

We started back into the work and continued until he was satisfied with all the finished pieces. There were four beautiful posts and four planks, two longer and two shorter. We had installed metal brackets in the posts, about thirty centimetres from the bottom. The smell of the stain was still strong, although the heat lamps had dried the posts and they weren't even sticky anymore. I felt tired and slumped down to the floor.

"Tired?" he asked, shaking his head. "Up to this point I was impressed at how hard you could work. You are a stubborn worker."

"I'm not tired," I lied. "I was just waiting to see what you wanted me to do next."

"Good, good. I like to hear that. We have one more job each to complete. Are you sure you can still work?"

"Yeah, no problem. I could go on for hours," I answered as I picked myself up off the floor.

"My job is to sweep and clean and oil all of the machines. Your job is to carry all of these pieces up to your room."

"My room?" I couldn't hide the confusion I felt.

"Well, we are not planning on having you sleep down here in the shop in your new bed."

"My new bed?"

"Yes. I told you that you would sleep better once we had finished with our work today. Your oma told us earlier that they had delivered our order. A new box spring, mattress, and bedspread. You are very lucky I stopped your oma from ordering the bedding that she wanted or you would have been sleeping on flowery sheets. Now, they are in your room, waiting for us to put everything together."

I didn't know what to say. I just stood there, holding on to one of the posts, speechless and not moving.

"It was not right for you to use that cot any longer. Boys grow when they sleep, and you would grow all crooked sleeping in that old cot. Now, you had better get moving. There is still work to be done."

I grabbed the post I was holding and cradled it gently in both arms. It was solid and heavy and smooth and beautiful to touch and see. I felt a wave of happiness surge up inside. I wanted to say something to him, to thank him or something, but . . . once again I just didn't have the words.

He had already moved to the far end of the shop, his back to me, and was using a hand vacuum to clean the sawdust off the floor.

"Grandfather," I called, but he couldn't hear me over the hum of the vacuum and didn't turn around, "thank you."

I headed out the door, careful not to bang the post against the door frame.

Seven

"Could everyone please take out their math textbooks and turn to page 157," Mr. Roberts announced to the class.

Without bothering to even look at the page, I raised my hand. "Mr. Roberts, I have a question."

"What a surprise, Jonathan. I suspected you would. The answer to your question is that, yes, you must do this work."

"But, sir, I —"

"— already covered this work in your old school," he said cutting me off and finishing the sentence. "It is truly remarkable that almost everything we have taken since you arrived three weeks ago you have already done."

"I'm pretty amazed myself. I guess those other schools were just more advanced and had better teachers, or something. Anyway, I don't think it's —"

"— fair that you should have to do this work," he again cut me off.

"That's right, it's not fair."

It was bad enough he kept on completing my sentences, but the really annoying part was that he was completing them correctly.

"Perhaps you would like to make a deal, Jonathan?"

"A deal?" I liked the sound of that, but somehow I wasn't sure I'd like this particular deal.

"Yes, Jonathan. I know how much you enjoy a good deal, and this is a truly good deal. If you can complete your end of the agreement, then you are excused from this entire section of the mathematics curriculum."

He walked very deliberately between the rows of desks to my seat. The others were all pretending to work. Maybe their eyes were on their books, but every ear in the place was aimed directly at us. Then he placed a set of stapled papers, maybe three or four sheets total, face down on my desk.

"Don't turn them over . . . yet. However, if you do not meet your end of the agreement, then you will need to work even harder than the rest of the class. Are you ready to be tested on this material?"

I looked up at him. I had half expected to see a smirk or even a full smile. But there was no expression on his face at all. It was a blank mask, a poker face.

"You're kidding me, right?" I asked.

"No kidding. Are you willing to take a chance? Do we have a deal or don't we?"

I looked at the sheets. I looked up at his face and then back down at the sheets. "No deal," I said quietly.

He turned away and started to walk back to his desk. I was steamed. He had got me, and in front of the whole class. I started to open my textbook when, like a bolt of lightning, I realized that he had walked away and left the test sitting on my desk! I slid down in my seat, trying to hide behind the kid in front of me. I could now look at the test, copy out all the questions, and work out the answers with a calculator. Then, tomorrow I could take the test and get perfect. I would get out of having to do any more work. We'd see who got the last laugh!

Quietly, I turned the test over. The first page was blank, probably to do rough work on. I turned to the next page. Blank. The next was blank and the back page was blank as well. I was thrown. Then, it hit me. This guy had just bluffed me, taken me. I didn't even want to look up. I knew he'd be sitting there with a smile on his face.

* * *

Lunch took longer than usual to arrive. I had struggled with the math problems and made almost no progress. I had backed myself into a corner on this one. There was no way I could go and ask Roberts for any help or else he'd know I was either a liar or stupid. He probably had both of those things figured out anyway.

I joined Stan and Vern, who were sitting at their usual table, off in the far corner.

Tommy wasn't there yet. He usually came a few minutes late. For the first few days I sat by myself at lunch. I felt naked, sitting there alone. It felt like everybody in the whole place, even the lunchroom supervisors, were staring at me like I was some sort of pathetic geek nobody would eat with.

We made small talk as they pulled out their lunches. Sandwiches wrapped in wax paper, thermos filled with soup or stew, fruit, and veggies. The common thing about townie lunches was that they were never fancy, but they were big.

"Hey, guys, I forgot my lunch again . Do you think you could loan me a couple of bucks?" I asked.

"I'm tapped out," said Stan, "but you can have one of my sandwiches."

"I've got two dollars," Vern said as he pulled the

crumpled bill out of his jeans pocket. "That makes nine dollars you owe me."

"And don't forget about my six," Stan added.

"I know, I know. Don't worry, I'm good for it. It's just that my grandparents don't have much money and they haven't decided about my allowance yet. I guess it's taking all their money just to take care of me . . ." I let the sentence trail away. They both looked away, embarrassed for my "poor" grandparents.

Vern reached over and put his hand on my shoulder. "It's okay. Pay me back when you can."

"And try to remember your lunch occasionally," Stan said.

"I'll try," I replied cheerfully.

Actually, I remembered my lunch every day. I remembered to take it from the fridge. I remembered to put it in my backpack. And I remembered to throw it in a ditch as I walked to school. I didn't want any healthy townie lunches.

"I'll be right back," I said as I headed for the cafeteria. A large Coke and an order of fries would just hit the spot. Waiting in line, I noticed Roberts in the teachers' express line. He saw me and smiled. Anybody else watching would have thought he was just being friendly, but I knew he was laughing at me. I was fuming as I sat back down at the table.

"Why does Roberts give me such a hard time?" I asked.

"Don't take it personal. He gives everybody a hard time," replied Vern. "Matter of fact, he gives the hardest times to the people he likes the most."

"Yeah, like Tommy," added Stan.

"Tommy?" I asked.

"Tommy has trouble with math, and Mr. Roberts

gives him extra time during lunch sometimes," Vern explained.

"Why does he need extra help? This stuff is easy," I lied.

"It's not 'cause he's stupid or anything," Vern said.

"And," continued Stan, "if you even hinted you thought he was, Tommy would pound on you something good."

Vern nodded. "Tommy's got some learning disabilities. Numbers are hard for him to understand. He has to work slower and longer and harder than most people. Sometimes he doesn't want to, but Mr. Roberts doesn't take no for an answer."

As we spoke, Tommy came across the lunchroom and took his seat at the table.

"How did it go?" Vern asked.

"Okay, I guess. The way he explains it, in little steps, it almost makes sense. By the time I'm finished the extra homework he gave me, I'm pretty sure I'll understand it."

"He gave you extra homework!" I said in amazement.

"Yeah, he gives me extra work almost every night," Tommy replied.

"What a jerk! Where does Roberts get off doing that?" I snarled, still mad at him for what he did to me.

Tommy put down his sandwich very deliberately. He finished chewing and swallowed what was in his mouth and then looked me squarely in the face.

"You know, Jonathan, you're still pretty new around here and you don't know nothing about nothing, so I'm not that mad at you, but get this straight. I don't want you to call him names anymore. At least not when I'm around."

I swallowed a fry that suddenly felt like a giant lump in my throat, then nodded. Tommy was wrong. I did know something. I knew enough not to get him mad.

"Lighten up will you, Tommy," said Vern. "You had a few choice names for Mr. Roberts the first time you met him."

"Yeah, Tommy," Stan reminded him, "tell Jonathan about your first meeting with Mr. Roberts."

Tommy's serious look quickly changed, and his familiar smile made the tension that was in the air vanish. "Well, he first talked to me at the end of a soccer game between our old school and Vista."

"Mr. Roberts is the coach of the Vista soccer team," added Vern.

"We won the game. I think the score was four to one and I'd scored two goals. I was only in Grade Six then, but I still played as a starter. Anyway, right after the game he called me over, congratulated me, and then started to tell me all the things I had done wrong or that I needed to work on."

"Do you remember the names you called him after that?" asked Vern.

"I can help you, if you forgot," added Stan, playfully.

"Why don't you two jerks shut up and let me continue with my story." Tommy's eyes flashed.

Vern and Stan saluted. Then Vern pretended to zipper his mouth, while Stan clamped both hands over his.

"I wasn't interested in hearing anything he had to say. I didn't even want to talk to anybody from Vista. I told him I was already good enough to score two goals against his team, and besides, if he was such a great coach, how come his team stank? He just walked away without saying a word. I thought that would be the end of him."

"That's when you called him all those . . . oops, I'm sorry. I'm not supposed to talk," Stan acknowledged.

Tommy continued. "As I was saying before I was interrupted by bozo, ten minutes later Mr. Roberts comes back over to me with Mr. Allison, our coach. Mr. Allison blasted me for being rude to a teacher, even if that teacher was from another school. He gave me a one-hour detention, starting right that minute, to be supervised by Mr. Roberts."

"You should have seen your face, Tommy. I enjoyed that more than winning the game that afternoon," chuckled Vern.

"So Mr. Roberts walked me down to the end of the field to serve my detention. He threw down a soccer ball and started to explain how he wanted me to shift my balance and learn to use my left foot. He said I was only a one-legged player. He made me take off my right shoe and practise shots. He put down pylons for me to dribble through, he strung up targets in the net, he made me hop on one foot. He explained things to me like nobody ever had before. This guy knew soccer. We didn't stop until it got dark."

"You got to understand, Jonathan," said Vern, "our old coach was a heck of a nice guy, but he didn't know anything about soccer."

"He used to just throw down the ball and tell us not to get hurt and to have fun," added Stan.

"Ever since then, after every game we played against Vista, Mr. Roberts would give me more advice or explain something. It was really strange being coached by the other side's coach."

"Just think," said Vern, "the worst beatings ever taken by Mr. Roberts's teams at Vista were because of the help he gave to Tommy."

"Yeah, Tommy was our best player and he always

played his best games with Mr. Roberts watching," added Stan.

"I'm looking forward to seeing Tommy play for Vista. When does the season start?" I asked innocently.

All at once the laughing and joking stopped. I didn't know what I'd said or done, but their strange reaction made me nervous.

Without another word, Tommy gathered up the litter that remained from his lunch, grabbed his bag, walked toward the garbage can, tossed in his trash, and left.

I turned to Vern. "What's wrong? What did I say?"

"Well, Jonathan, you know Tommy likes Mr. Roberts and he loves soccer, but he ain't never going to play for Vista."

"That's right. He doesn't like the kids or the school. Vista was always the enemy, and since we came here, it's not like they tried to make us feel welcome or that we belong," said Stan.

I could agree with that. I didn't feel part of this place, either. But, then again, I didn't really feel a part of any place. Just then the five-minute bell rang. We gathered our stuff and moved toward the crush of kids heading for class.

I made a mental note to go and find Tommy before the end of the day. I'd offer to "help" him with his math homework. Since Mr. Roberts had explained the math to Tommy, maybe I could figure out how to do it by watching him do his homework.

Eight

There was an unreal quality to living with my grandparents. The days were predictable, made up of regular, almost ritualistic activities. I could set my watch by what was happening. It wasn't necessarily bad, just very different from what I was used to.

Living with my father was a lot of things, but it was never predictable, mostly because of the way he earned his living. He jokingly called it, "fishing." But there were other names for it: running a confidence racket, grafting, scamming, game playing, flimflamming. But no matter the name, it was the same game. He made his money doing things that were either almost legal or downright illegal.

He didn't break into houses, or steal cars, or point a gun at people. These were the activities of petty criminals. My father didn't ever think of himself as a lawbreaker, but as a skilled professional. He used his brains and his words to convince people they should give him their money. And he was very good at it.

To pull off the different scams, my father had to be a terrific actor. Watching him at work was like watching a TV show. Actually, our whole life seemed like some made-for-TV movie.

My father loved pulling off the big cons. His favourite involved selling fake franchises. He'd set himself up as a businessman who was selling the distribution rights to a wonderful product that would make everybody rich. Sometimes it was a real product, but most often it was a miracle that lived only in my father's imagination.

He would lease an office, get business cards printed, leaflets distributed, furniture rented, and contracts created. This involved a lot of money up front, but there was a lot of money to be made. On the big night, he would be up on stage in front of a packed audience.

He said he got his best ideas reading the headlines of those tabloid newspapers. "Always know what the suckers want, what type of bait the fish are biting before you put your line in the water," he'd say. Whether he was promoting a cosmetic to remove wrinkles, a cure for baldness, stronger nails, a miracle cleaner, a better mousetrap, hypnosis to stop smoking, or a remedy for arthritis, he was amazing to watch. Although I knew it was all a big fake, he was so convincing even I couldn't help but believe him.

Throughout the audience he had planted people who were part of the scam. They would claim to have made fast and easy money selling the product, or to have been cured by using it.

In the weeks after the presentation my father would work long hours at his office dealing with the people who were tripping over one another to give him their money.

The most important element was deciding when to get out and make a break. It had to be timed to get as much money as possible but to get out before the bills came due or somebody saw through the scam.

When we made our move, it would be in the dead of night. Investors who called in would get a message on the answering machine informing them we were closed for a "medical emergency." A similar sign was on the locked office door. They'd be sidetracked for a few days while we put half the country behind us. We'd leave behind a deserted office — with the rent overdue, of course — filled with expensive leased furniture as well as leaflets and brochures that had never been paid for.

And fake names. We had used so many different names that I sometimes stumbled over my real one.

My role in these cons was to do exactly as my father had instructed me. Just like writing a play, he had created a character for me and written lines that were mine to say. It was essential that I never deviated from the original script. One wrong word could cause the whole thing to fall down, and we could end up caught. My father drilled this into me time and time again.

When we had money, we lived well. First class was his class, my father would say. Money never stayed with my father very long. Every cent we had was spent on the best. But it also meant we often had nothing. Sometimes there wasn't even enough money to buy food. At these times my father would resort to quick moneymakers.

The simplest of these cons involved a mustard bottle. My father would have me walk up to a well-dressed businessman who was carrying a briefcase or suitcase. Without him noticing, I'd squirt mustard on him. Then, innocently, I would point out the mess. When the man put down his case to clean the mustard, my father would swoop down and take it, while I quickly moved away to our prearranged safe spot.

Another, less-risky dodge involved credit cards. In every city there's a network of con men. My father could always find people with stolen credit cards to sell. Often these were taken right out of the mail, before the person had seen or signed them, and those were worth a fortune. These cards could be bought for a few hundred dollars. Then the new owner of the card could run up thousands of dollars of merchandise in just a few hours. Some of the purchases were returned for cash refunds, others were sold to "fences," and some we just kept.

No matter how successful the con, when it was completed, it was time to move on. We took with us what we could pack in a bag or throw in the back of the car, leaving everything, and everybody behind.

One time, when I was about eleven, my father tried to make it at a "straight" job. He worked as a salesman. He joked that it involved basically the same set of skills, but this way he got to take away people's money legally. He was a very good salesman.

We lived in a little place called Tupper Lake. It's in New York State, away from any of the big cities. Most evenings my father was home early. I'd have supper on the table, waiting for him when he came in the door. I always made sure the house was clean and tidy. I fixed up my room and put posters on all the walls and even on the ceiling.

It was just a little house, wedged on a small strip of land between the highway and the lake. Out our back door we could hear water lapping, while out the front the cars and trucks whizzing by sounded like they were driving right through our living room. At night the big lumber trucks, alone on the roads, would roar by, almost shaking me out of my bed.

After a while, though, even that noise came to feel like home and was no more disturbing than the sound of the waves washing up on the shore.

It was strange to be in one school so long. I started to hang around with some kids and thought some of them were even becoming my friends. It looked like I might spend the whole year in one school.

It wasn't going to happen. My father came home from work one day and said he'd had enough, that it was time to move. He didn't go to work the next morning and I didn't go to school. I carefully took down all my posters. I hardly ripped any of the corners. I rolled them all up and packed them with our stuff. I still have those posters. Someday I might put them back up.

Within two days we'd sold all our stuff and were gone.

I guess I couldn't really blame him. He was right. It was time to get moving. I was getting bored. We needed some excitement. I didn't blame him. Really.

We left Tupper Lake just after the sun came up. We drove all day and into the night. When I woke up we had arrived at Uncle Arthur's. Uncle Arthur wasn't really my uncle. He was a good friend of my father's, and my father didn't have many friends.

Each winter, usually around Christmas, we'd head south for a few weeks or months of sun. On the way down we would always stop to see Uncle Arthur. Arthur ran a gas station along one of the big interstate highways.

My father told me Arthur had decided that the very best way to run a scam was from behind a legitimate business. He hustled the tourists that migrated up and down the interstate like salmon swimming along a stream.

Tourists are a favourite target of con men. They're often tired and confused, and they carry plenty of money.

To attract the "fish," you need the right kind of bait. In this case, for a hundred miles in both directions along the interstate, gigantic billboards advertised The Cleanest Restrooms in the South, Cheap Gas, Outdoor Playground.

Arthur was proud of those billboards. He said he had summed up, in ten simple words, what every father, mother, and kid thought was most important.

And the signs were right. The gas was a tenth of a cent cheaper, the washrooms were spotless, and the playground was a delight.

When I was little, I'd spend hours there. Every second car that came along brought another wave of kids to play with me. It really didn't matter if they were nice kids or bad ones. In ten or fifteen minutes they would be gone, replaced by the next swell of playmates. In that playground I learned one of the most important lessons in life. Whether you liked somebody or not, they'd be gone soon enough. And there was nothing you could do about it.

To top it all off, Uncle Arthur was friendly, helpful, smiling, gentle, and bumbling. My father would say the most important thing for a con man was genuineness, and when you could fake that, everything else came easy. Uncle Arthur also thought it was important to appear "simple." He said people trusted people who weren't very bright. Arthur was bright, bright enough to act dumb.

Uncle Arthur treated me really well. He cooked my favourite foods, gave me special treats and toys, read me bedtime stories, and tucked me in at night. He may not have been my real uncle, but he was my family.

I didn't have anybody except my father, so Uncle Arthur was even more special. Sometimes my father's girlfriends tried to act like they were family, but I knew to just wait them out. It wasn't like they'd be around for long. None of them lasted more than a couple of months.

Uncle Arthur had a couple of kids. They were all grown up now, and he didn't know where they were. I know that hurt him. His wife had just taken the kids one day and moved away from him. Uncle Arthur hadn't seen them for twenty years. He said that if they came in to get gas, he could serve them without even realizing who they were.

Uncle Arthur looked forward to our visits. He and my father respected each other's abilities and would compare notes. My father explained to me how Uncle Arthur ran his cons. Uncle Arthur would joke that if you were ever thirsty you could drink straight out of his pumps. What he meant was that he watered down his gas. Motorists paid for gas and also got a dose of water included.

He was like a chemist, figuring out how much water he could add to the holding tanks so he could get the most profit but still get the cars to roll away. He said one tank of watered-down gas wouldn't hurt any car. He would joke that they should be paying him extra for washing their engines from the inside out.

He had also "fixed" the little price wheels on the pumps. When the pump indicated a dollar, the motorist really got only ninety cents worth of liquid. There were inspectors who checked on both the quality of the gas and the workings of the pumps. Uncle Arthur said that through clean living, good luck and a few small but well-placed bribes, he had never had any trouble.

Uncle Arthur was a good mechanic and knew how to fix cars. This also meant he knew how to unfix a car. He would quickly size up a car and its occupants as it rolled up to the pumps. Then he'd decide who to hook and who to let swim away. He liked expensive cars, especially ones with out-of-state or foreign plates, driven by well-dressed people with clean hands. These were signs that meant they had money, likely wouldn't be sticking around to cause trouble, and probably didn't know much about engines. Uncle Arthur would say, "You don't see no mechanics driving around in no Mercedes."

My father would point out that Arthur drove a Mercedes, but he was really much more than a mechanic. He was an artist.

A car would pull in, and the kids would pile off to the playground while the parents went to check out the washrooms. Uncle Arthur, under the hood to check the oil, would adjust or disconnect or snap some part of the engine. After that, the car wouldn't start, or would roar like a monster, or get half a mile down the road and then die. Then, he would tow the car back or just push it into his garage. It'd be easy to fix the problem. After all, there was no guesswork involved. He knew what was wrong because he'd just made it wrong.

While the car was being worked on, Uncle Arthur would arrange for the people to be comfortable. He had an air-conditioned lounge with a big-screen TV, cozy chairs, and a view overlooking the playground. He gave them a snack and cold drinks ("Usually I charge for these, folks, but you've had a bad day") and told them everything would be all right.

Hours later he'd give them a bill for work not done or needed. The car worked, and the tourists gladly paid the money. They considered themselves lucky to have had their car repaired by such a nice, honest man.

Occasionally somebody would question the repairs.

This wasn't a problem for Uncle Arthur. It was the mark of a careful con to always have his plan backed up.

It was at Uncle Arthur's that I first played an active part in a scam. My father told me that we were going to play a game and pretend to be other people. This game, with yearly changes, became one of our regular cons when we traveled south. It helped to finance our vacations.

Uncle Arthur would pull out an old beaten-up car with out-of-state plates and park it just away from the pumps. My father, dressed in old clothes, would be under the hood, "working" on the car. I was also dressed in old clothes. Uncle Arthur would give me a cue to tell me which cars were the targets. My job was to walk up to that vehicle and try to sell the occupants one of my toys "because we need the money to get home to our ma, who's sick."

After I walked away, Uncle Arthur would explain that our car was broken down and needed a part worth $46.50 (or $89 or $116, depending on what he thought he could get out of the sucker). He'd even offer to put the part in for free because he "felt so bad for the troubles of this poor man and his son."

And people gave money. Lots of money, often more than what we needed to fix the car. On our best day, hitting about one car every fifteen minutes, we caught thirty-one fish. They left behind $1485.00. The split was two-fifths for my father, two-fifths for Uncle Arthur, and one-fifth for me. That worked out to my share being worth $297.00. For one day's work. Not bad money for a ten-year-old.

Nine

It was zero minus two minutes. Two minutes until the end of school. Day nineteen. Like a convict chalking up the days on the wall of his cell, I kept a mental note of time already served. I hunched over my desk to finish up the last of my work. The room was quiet. I heard footsteps and looked up to see Mr. Roberts standing over me.

He bent down and quietly spoke in my ear. "Jonathan, I want you to stay after school for a few minutes. I have things to discuss with you."

Without acknowledging him, I turned back to my work. There were times when his voice, with that soft accent, almost sounded like music. Right now wasn't one of those times. He probably wanted to talk to me about my test results.

Over the past couple of weeks he'd been all over me like a bad smell. While the rest of the class worked away on their regular assignments, he had been giving me "standardized tests." He said he was trying to learn my strengths and weaknesses. He said that everybody else had taken these tests at some time in their school history and that those results were on their student records. I didn't have a student record. Or, more correctly, I probably had twenty-four or twenty-five different student records.

When we moved, it had to be done quickly and quietly and so that nobody could trace us. One day I was Jonathan Moore, living in one part of the country, and two days later I was Joey Millen or Jake Miller or Joshua Morrison, living on the other side of the continent.

Even if all my records could be gathered together, there'd be a lot of gaps. I would often skip tests. If I didn't want to go to school, I would just stay home and watch TV or spend the day in a video arcade.

At times, a teacher or principal would try to give me a hard time over the skipped school or missed tests. My father would take care of things. He had a way of handling people. With some he'd be so charming they'd be eating out of his hand. If the teacher was female, particularly if she was young, he would turn on the charm. With male teachers he would treat them like long lost buddies. With some, usually the older ones, he would talk about the problems in raising a "motherless child." He could turn on the tears as easily as turning on a tap. Usually by the end of the interview the teacher would be crying right along with him.

He also had one more angle. I didn't even like to see this one. He got plain nasty. He would question the teacher's skills, dedication, intelligence, training, and right to know. He would turn the whole discussion into an exercise in what a terrible teacher they were. He would speak to the principal, write to the school trustee, threaten to have the teacher fired.

The first time he ever did this, the teacher was a mean, nasty man named Crozier. That man deserved the hard time my father gave him. My father seemed to enjoy the whole thing until two months later, Mr. Crozier "retired." From that point on, any time a

teacher caused us any concern, or questioned any
thing, Dad would play this angle.

I saw up close what this could do to teachers. The
would begin to look tired, like they hadn't bee
sleeping. Often they would almost stop teaching th
class, like other things were taking their attention
Supply teachers would take their place on more an
more days. And, they would leave me alone. On
teacher wouldn't even talk to me. They acted scare
of me. More correctly, I knew they were scared o
him.

In the end I even stopped telling him when I ha
problems at school. I was more afraid of what he migh
do to the teacher than what any teacher might do t
me. I don't know who, or what, or when, but som
teacher, at some time, must have done something ba
to my father. Now, every teacher he faced paid for it
He said he'd never met a teacher he couldn't "teac
a lesson to." If he ever met Mr. Roberts, they'd be
pretty even match.

My thoughts were interrupted by the 3:30 bell. M
classmates quickly packed up their things. Tomm
gave me a nod as he exited. Soon we were alone in th
classroom, just the two of us, Mr. Roberts and me, an
the air was still. I got up and moved to his desk. Th
sooner we started, the sooner I could leave.

"Well, Jonathan," he started, "I've had an opportu
nity to examine the results of all those tests I've bee
having you complete. You have been a mystery sinc
you came to my class. A student without a past. I mus
admit I really enjoy solving a good mystery."

Well, I would really enjoy your taking a flying leap
I thought, but you don't always get what you want.

"With these scores, some of the mystery has bee
solved. But, other mysteries have been created. In al

my years of teaching I have never seen anything like these results."

He opened his big green day book and flipped to the back. He ran his finger down the column to find the results marked beside my name.

"You really enjoy reading, don't you, Jonathan?"

"I guess. When there's nothing else happening, I read."

"Well, I can assume you have enjoyed a great deal of time when nothing was happening, because you have developed excellent reading skills. You are reading years above your level. You didn't enjoy our novel study though, did you?"

"Well . . . no. I thought the book was . . ."

"Boring?" he added to complete my sentence.

That was the word I had in mind, but I wasn't giving him the satisfaction of guessing right. "I was going to say stupid."

"I'm not surprised, Jonathan. It was unfortunate, and I apologize, but I simply didn't know enough about you to place you anywhere but in the middle group. In the future, you will be in a group of one, working on your own."

I nodded. I think he was telling me something good, but I'd have to wait to see if it meant more work.

"Now, let's look at your spelling. As good as you are as a reader, I expected your spelling marks to be higher. Don't get me wrong. Your spelling is fine, just not in line with your reading level."

He turned the page and ran his finger down the left column. I knew that my name was at the very bottom. Late entries in a class always ended up out of alphabetical order at the bottom of the page.

He shook his head and muttered something under his breath. It almost sounded like a curse.

"What did you say, Mr. Roberts?"

"Nothing, or nothing that I should have said or should repeat." He paused and again shook his head. "You have the most extreme math profile I have ever seen. So extreme that I remarked your test. Three times. Each time I got the same results, no mistake. Judging from these results, I can't quite decide whether you are severely learning disabled or a complete genius who was just playing with the results. I just don't know what to think. Instead of wasting any more time, I'm just going to give you the results."

He moved his chair from behind the desk so that he was sitting right beside me.

"On long division, fractions, and multiplication, your scores are grades below level. Interesting, it looked like somebody tried to teach you a simplified method for division, one I teach myself. Unfortunately, it looks like it was badly taught."

I thought it best not to tell him that Tommy had been my teacher when I was "helping" him with his extra homework.

"On the problem-solving and probability section, I know you're good. I just don't know how good. You answered every single question perfectly. Actually, you answered one question better than perfect. At first I thought you were wrong, because your answer was different than the marking sheets. When I looked closely, very closely, I started to see the logic of your answer. After a great deal of work I was able to see that you had the right answer, just at a much higher level of logic. You were more right than anybody would expect a Grade Eight student, or even a Grade Eight teacher, to ever be." His voice had got higher, faster, and louder as he spoke.

He looked back at his book and again started to

shake his head. Then he looked up and stared straight into my eyes.

"Your moving from place to place would explain the gaps. I don't know how to explain the extraordinarily high scores. I do suspect two things, however. One, you do have some idea about why you scored so high, and two, you're not about to tell me."

I tried to keep my face from revealing any hint of emotion. I just shrugged my shoulders. "I don't know what you mean, Mr. Roberts. Can I go now?"

"Yes, you can go now. Even if I don't know why, I do know that you will be joining Tommy for additional help in those areas where you have difficulties. I'll be speaking to your grandparents and sharing the results." Mr. Roberts took a deep breath. "Is there anything else you want to say, Jonathan?"

"Nope. I just want to go."

* * *

Walking home, I had time to think. I had almost wanted to explain things to Mr. Roberts, to help solve the mystery. He was a major pain in the butt, but I almost liked the guy. Almost.

He was right about the parts he had guessed. Going to school, and not going to school, the way I had, it was easy to understand the gaps. Between moving from place to place, missing school, copying from other people's work, using my calculator, and having my dad cover for me, I had avoided a lot of schoolwork. Teachers didn't know what I knew or didn't know.

With the things I was good at, it was like everything else in life; practice makes perfect. I had spent a lot of time around racetracks, card games, and dice tables. You learn about the odds, the probabilities. I know what the chances are of drawing a ten in blackjack when there are twenty cards left in the deck and six are tens. I know that a seven is three times as likely as an eleven in craps. I know the odds are always against you in roulette. I know when you draw one card in poker, looking for a card to fill a flush, the odds are you'll lose your rent money.

We lost a lot of rent money. My father was one great con man but one crummy gambler. You can't talk cards or dice into being something they're not. It was bad enough when he lost the money we had, but even worse when he lost what we didn't have.

Professional gamblers are bad losers but even worse winners when they don't get what they are owed. Broken promises and bad debts became broken legs and battered knees. When we ran from them, like I figured my father was now, we ran hard.

All of my life was an exercise in problem solving. Just getting by was problem enough. My father was always "schooling" me in how to run a scam. He would explain and test me on situations, things that might happen. Unlike the problems in a math book, solving these problems meant the difference between eating and going hungry, having a place to sleep that night or having to leave town in the dead of night or being able to stay a little longer.

According to those tests, I'd obviously learned quite a bit. Maybe things I'd be better off never knowing. I knew how to cheat people. I guess maybe it isn't right.

My father got mad at me when I mentioned things like that. As far as he is concerned, there are only two types of people in the world, "those that take and those that get taken." He would say that he didn't know if I had enough guts to be a good con man. I thought maybe my problem was the complete opposite. I had too many guts. They would gurgle, make loud noises, get tied up in knots, feel like I'd swallowed a rock, and crowd into my throat like I was going to throw up.

Not always, though. Some of the cons I could play pretty well, but others were just too scary. The ones that scared me the most had me up front in a scam that didn't just bend the law, but shattered it into little pieces. When we did a con like that my father always had an escape plan worked out. If something went wrong, I knew what to do, where to go, and what to say. We practised the way out. A couple of times it did go wrong. Once it exploded all over my face, and I was caught.

The police didn't know what to do with me. It wasn't every day that they came across an eleven-year-old con man. My father had got away clean. I was a curiosity. It was him they wanted, and they didn't even have a name.

At first a bunch of policemen talked to me. They tried to joke around, be my friend, bring me donuts to eat. When this didn't work, they tried to scare me. Just as my father had predicted, they tried "good cop, bad cop." One guy tried to frighten the daylights out of me and then left. His partner then acted super nice and suggested we talk before the other guy returned. I had to work hard not to smile. It was reassuring that things were going just like my father had forewarned. He had told me they wouldn't hurt me, no matter what they said. They couldn't throw an eleven-year-old into jail. He said, "Just stay quiet, don't give any information up front. I'll come and get you."

After the policemen, came the social workers. They were kinder and gentler than the police. They had on sad faces of concern. They tried to trick me into giving answers. They weren't that smart. Certainly not smart enough to trick me into anything. When they had grown tired, it was time for the foster parents.

I was brought to a big old house. There was a couple who lived there and took care of kids who didn't have any other place to go. There I was given food, the first food I'd had since the donuts at the station, and a change of clothes. Then, like we had practised it, I started to cry and tell a story. The crying was easy. I was scared. I figured I'd lost my father. Still, I gave my story, the way he'd told me.

Whenever we practised anything, I had learned to deliver the lines exactly like my father wanted. Just the way he had thought of them. He said there was an exactly perfect way to say things, and, as long as I followed the script, there wouldn't be any problems. I believed him. I believed him so much I didn't know what to say if things went off course. I could always think of two or three or four things to say, but none of them was exactly perfect. Instead, I just got flustered and stuttered and stammered and didn't say much of anything. There were times I even had the same problem with my name. I had used so many different names over the years that I stumbled on my real one.

This time, for the social workers and foster parents, it came off just the way it was supposed to. I gave them a false name. Jodie Moog. Fake names should always have the same initials as real names to make them easier to remember. I told them I didn't know where I lived but described a motel room that could have been any motel. I told them I lived with my mother and her boyfriend and gave more false names. I told them I was forced to be part of the con. I told them how glad I was to be there. Then, I went to bed.

For the next two days I stayed in the foster home. I stuck with my story, cooperated, and cried. The crying wasn't part of the script. I just couldn't stop it. And I waited for my father to come.

The third night, as I was looking out my bedroom window after everybody in the house had gone to sleep, I saw the signal.

At the end of the street a car was parked, and every minute the inside light flashed on and off. Ticking like a clock.

Not bothering to change out of my pyjamas I tip-toed down the stairs. I skipped over the fifth and third last steps. They both squeaked. I had practised moving around the house with my eyes closed, so that I could get around better in the dark. Barefooted, I moved to the front door. I slipped off the chain lock, turned the knob, opened the door, and squeezed through the opening. I closed the door gently, letting it softly kiss the door frame.

My feet flew down the front path and along the street. I opened the door and hurled myself inside. "What took you, Jonnie?" was all he said as I settled into the seat. I was gasping to catch my breath. The burst of speed after not daring to even breathe had left me winded. "Did you tell them anything?" I shook my head. "Good, good. Maybe you got what it takes after all."

He started the engine, and we raced away into the night.

Ten

Lately, I'd taken to coming straight home from school each day. My grandparents were thrilled I was following their orders.

What they didn't know was that I didn't dare show my face in the video arcade anymore. It was the only place in town I could hang out, but now I owed too many people too much money. It wasn't a fortune. A few bucks borrowed here, a lost game or bet there, an unpaid tab for food at the snack bar. Little by little it all added up, and people were getting angry because I wasn't paying them what they were owed.

People get their shorts in a knot over a few bucks. I never figured this would amount to any sort of problem. I thought I'd be long gone by now. I couldn't believe it. It was almost the end of January, and I was still here.

Coming in through the back door, after a hard day at school, I found my grandmother sitting at the kitchen table and was surprised to find her crying. It was a soft whimper, just a few tears, one still running down her cheek. She tried to hide her crying from me. I hated when people cried. It made me get all nervous inside.

She quickly rose from the table and rushed over to

the sink, where she rattled around a few dishes. Her back was to me.

"Jonathan, you are here early. You must have run half the way home. Would you like me to get you a drink or fix you an after-school snack? You must be hungry. I am so happy you are eating better these days."

One of the reasons I was eating better was that I didn't have any choice. Nobody would lend me any more money for food.

"Thanks. A drink would be nice." Actually, a Coke would go down well, but I knew my choice would be limited to seven or eight different kinds of fruit and vegetable juices. It's amazing how carrot juice kind of grows on you after a while.

"What kind of juice would you like?" she asked.

"Any kind would be fine. Why don't I help myself. Do you need any help with the dishes?" I enquired.

"No, no. That is all right, but thank you for your offer."

I could still hear the catch of tears in her throat. I took two glasses off the shelf and poured two glasses of juice, and set them down on the table.

"I've poured one for you, too. I know you'll want to ask me a lot of questions about how my day went," I said.

Without facing me, she took her apron and dried her hands and wiped her face. She turned and smiled. She walked over and sat down at the table beside me. Her eyes were puffy and red. It looked like she had been crying for a while. I didn't like to see her like this. Her tears unnerved me. I remembered the times I'd found my mother crying and how powerless I was to help.

"Jonathan . . . you are a very kind boy. And you were a very cute baby. I want to show you."

I had been so busy watching my grandmother, I hadn't noticed a small book sitting on the table. The cover was light blue, and there was a silver title in fancy writing on the front. *Baby's First Year.*

She moved her chair right beside mine and then opened the book. On the first page was a picture of a newborn baby, and under the picture was written:

Name: Jonathan Nicholas Moore
Day of Birth: Monday, January 23
Time of Birth: 3:58 A.M.
Mother: Christina Moore (née van Gees)
Father: David Moore

I felt numb inside. This was about me. I didn't know what to say.

"That is your mother's writing, Jonathan. She had such a delicate, flowing handwriting. Just like her. Page after page of writing. She talks about her little baby, her Jonathan. You can feel the love she felt for you coming right through the pages. I do not imagine you can even remember seeing this book."

I picked up the book and held it. It seemed somehow familiar, but it was so long ago.

"When your mother died, we came to get you and the few belongings the two of you had. There was not really much to take. This book, some clothes, a few of your toys. I thought we could leave some things, but your opa insisted we take anything and everything that would remind us of your mother. They are up in the attic in a trunk. I have not looked at those things for years. Later, when you are ready, we can look through everything."

My chest felt tight, there was a knot in my stomach, and my throat was dry. I felt my lower lip start to quiver like I was going to cry. I wanted to turn the page and to look and look at the book, but I was too scared.

She took her arm and cradled my head on her shoulder.

"It is all right to cry, Jonathan," she said softly. "I have been crying myself. All afternoon. I miss your mother so much. I missed being there for her, helping with her baby, being your oma. We have all missed . . . so much."

She began to sob. I could hear it starting from deep in her chest, and it grew louder as it travelled up her throat and escaped from her lips. I heard the sobbing become even louder before I realized it was me crying. Tears streamed down my face and tasted of salt as they rolled into the corners of my mouth. We cried together for a long time. I couldn't remember the last time I had cried like this.

After a while she dabbed her eyes and then mine with the corner of her apron.

"I want to tell you about your mother, about my daughter. There is so much that you do not know. She was a wonderful person, a truly wonderful person. But, before you get to know her more, you must first get to know Jonathan. Let us turn the page now and look back," she said, her arm still around my shoulders.

***

Later, alone in my room, I went over and over the pages of the book.

It was eerie. I was reading about this little baby boy and trying to make the connection that this was me. Me. Me with a stuffed bear named Samuel tucked under my sleeping head. Me who sat up at four months, rolled over at five months, crawled at eight months, and took my first steps at eleven months. Me whose first word was ball, who called a pillow a pico, and a stroller a dodo. Me who was described as "always happy and smiling but very, very stubborn."

And the pictures! Smiling and happy in the bathtub, crawling down a hall, wearing a big baseball cap, with Samuel the bear. Standing with my mother, hand in hand, taking those first steps.

My mother. She was a beautiful woman. Soft and smiling. I ran my fingers over her picture, almost like I could touch her. She looked just like I remembered her, although it still seemed more as if I had dreamed her than ever really seen her. She was smiling.

Her eyes looked like mine, but even more like her mother's, my grandmother. We all shared the same blue eyes. I wondered if she could see me now.

My grandparents had lived in this house for forty years. My mother had grown up under this same roof I was sitting under. I guess that made her a townie, too.

My dad would speak about her. We had no pictures. It was almost as if he took her death as a personal insult. Almost like he was thinking, "the nerve of her to go and die on me," even though he had left her, left us, years before she died.

For me it was almost the complete opposite. For years I thought that maybe she had died because of something I did, or something I said, or maybe because I wasn't a good enough boy.

I never told anybody that she was dead. At each new school, with each new group of kids, I tried to keep it a secret. I felt ashamed and embarrassed. Even the word "Mother." When I try to say it, my tongue goes funny like it's a word from some foreign language I never learned to speak. Or maybe I'd learned but forgotten long ago.

Mother.

We missed so much.

Eleven

My grandmother and I were sitting in the kitchen together. It was my favourite place in the whole house. It was always warm from the fire in the corner stove and filled with the smell of cooking or baking. It reminded me of being in Uncle Arthur's kitchen. I was helping her peel and cut vegetables for the *hutspot.*

She strolled over to the cupboard, removed two mugs, and poured two cups of coffee from the pot on the stove. It was thick, rich Dutch coffee and like none I'd ever tasted before. I once drank a full cup. He had warned me it was strong but not just how strong. Stubbornly I had forced down the whole cup and couldn't sleep for hours after going to bed that night. I sat by my window, looking for the signal, until well past two in the morning.

"Jonathan, can you please take your opa a cup of coffee?"

"In the den?" I asked apprehensively.

"Yes, in the den. I imagine you have been wondering what he does in there each evening."

I nodded.

"Go in with this coffee. Ask your opa to explain."

I took the cup of coffee and started walking from the kitchen.

"And, Jonathan, you better knock very loud. He is

a little deaf always but a lot deaf when he is in there. If he does not answer, just go in anyway. The smell of that coffee could wake up a dead man, so I am sure it will snap him out of his trance."

I walked toward the den with a sense of excitement and trepidation. The door was always closed. I had never been in there, and no one had ever, before this, asked me if I wanted to go in. I didn't even recall ever seeing my grandmother in there. I was getting more and more comfortable in the house, but that room made me nervous.

The den was off the dining room, behind a big polished wooden door. Almost every afternoon when I came home from school, my grandfather was in there. And each evening, around my bedtime, he would say goodnight to me and again retreat to the den and close the door behind him.

At night, lying in my bed in the dark, when I couldn't get to sleep, I could hear him down there. Even with both the den and my bedroom doors closed, I could hear him. It's funny how much farther voices travel in the quiet of the night air. Sounds you normally wouldn't even notice are as clear as a bell. I could hear him talking to himself, or laughing out loud, or cursing, or even cheering. I had no idea what he was doing, but it was more than a little spooky.

As I approached the door, I could hear him talking. I knocked. There was no answer. I knocked again, this time louder. I heard him laugh, but there was still no answer. I took a deep breath, turned the knob, pushed the door open, and took one small step into the room.

He sat in a chair, facing a desk, his back angled away from me. On the desk sat a computer. Not just a regular home computer, though. In a glance I could see a high-resolution colour monitor, hard drive with capacity for two types of disks, a laser printer, mouse, joystick, and more than enough software to stock a small computer store.

I was overwhelmed. I was shocked. In a house without a dishwasher, VCR, power lawn mower, answering machine, food processor, CD player, cellular phone, or even a TV, the computer stood out like a beacon in the night. I quickly looked around the room. Who knows, maybe this is where they stashed the big-screen TV.

His fingers moved from the keyboard and he turned to face me.

"Jonathan, and coffee. Two very welcome, but unexpected, surprises. Please come in out of the doorway. Sit for a minute while I finish my thought."

He turned back to the computer. His fingers flew over the keyboard. It was fascinating to watch those enormous hands, missing finger bits and all, racing across the keys. I sat down in a chair and continued my visual inspection of the room.

The computer and printer sat on a large wooden desk. The desk was a warm, soft red colour, shiny and polished. It looked smooth to the touch. There was no wide-screen TV. There wasn't space. The walls were lined floor to ceiling with bookshelves overflowing with books and papers. There was a matching chair to the one I sat in. They were soft and overstuffed, the kind you don't sit on as much as *in*. Between the chairs was a long black leather chesterfield, worn and sagging in the middle. Scattered around the room was a series of small end tables and on each was a chessboard, the pieces either on or beside the boards, as though the games were in progress.

Turning my gaze back to where my grandfather was

sitting, I was startled to find that he had stopped his work and was watching me, a smile on his face.

"There is certainly a lot to study in my study, isn't there, Jonathan?"

I nodded.

"You must be curious," he said.

Again, I nodded.

"There is much to see in here, so I am not sure where to begin. Perhaps I will start with my books and end with the computer, my baby."

He rose from his chair. The room was not very large and already crowded, so when he stood he seemed to fill almost all the remaining space. Sometimes I lost touch with just how huge he was, but in a closed space like this, he was enormous. I bet he never lost a fight in his life.

"Around you, on every shelf, are friends whom I have spent time with. These friends talk to me about religion, agriculture, mathematics, famous literary works, poetry, engineering, the universe, geography, oceanography, animal science, medicine, psychology, sociology, and my very favourite, philosophy. Right now I am reading a book about fuzzy logic. I never thought that logic could be fuzzy, but I am learning that much of what I thought I knew was not right. Each day I read and try to leave a little wiser. I notice that you like to read. I would like you to feel free to come in here anytime . . . and I do mean anytime, and browse through my books. A book is best when it is shared. You can take them away or stay right here and read. If you choose to stay, I can tell you from experience that the couch is very comfortable, maybe too comfortable. I often drift to sleep there, book in hand."

I could picture him lying there, his feet hanging

over the end, the springs of the couch groaning under his weight, a book almost hidden in his huge hands. I had never heard him say more than a few words before, and I was thrown by the length of his description.

"And, while I gladly invite you to share my books, I ask you not to disturb my chessboards. Do you play chess?"

"No, I never learned how." I didn't mention that my dad had taught me a lot of games with cards and dice. "I've never seen anybody else in here. Whom do you play chess with?"

"Well, right now, I have six different games going on with six different players. Come and I will introduce you."

He moved to the first board and motioned me over. Half the pieces sat neatly beside the board. It looked about even between black and white pieces.

"In this game I am playing the black. My opponent, or as I would prefer to think of him, my partner, is Mr. Fredrick Tower. Mr. Tower, prior to his retirement, was a professor of mathematics at Queen's University. He is an excellent player. His style of play is very imaginative and creative. Moves that look, on the surface, like mistakes, are usually very complicated traps. Unfortunately, Mr. Tower has recently had medical difficulties, which have left him bound to his hospital bed. Fortunately, this has not interfered with our game together."

"Do you bring the board to the hospital to play?"

"Oh, no. He lives very far away from here, in Kingston. I have never been to Kingston. In fact, I have never even met Mr. Tower."

"But . . . but, if he can't come here and you don't go there, and you've never met him, how can you play chess together?" I asked, totally confused.

"Oh, Jonathan. I am sorry for sounding so mystical. We play by mail. Here, I am just mailing my next move," he replied with a soft chuckle.

He handed me a postcard. On the back was a name and address. The only message was written in big black letters.

Nxe4

His explanation really didn't clear up anything. "What does that mean?"

"That is algebraic notation. It is like chess short-hand. I am saying to my partner that I wish to move my knight to square e4 to capture his piece that is presently in possession of that square."

He then went on to explain the chess notation, the different games and the players he was playing. One player was in France, another in New York, one in Cuba, one just a few miles away, and the last was in Russia.

He stopped at each table and described the game in progress, his strategy, and that of the opponent.

He was particularly pleased with the game he described last, with Mr. Boris Alexandria.

"This game is my most challenging. Mr. Alexandria is always my greatest challenge. In the eighteen years we have played together, I have yet to win or even draw a game. Until now. I believe I am in a position to play him to a draw."

After he said this, he rushed up, grabbed me, and started dancing me around the board, my feet off the ground as he held me around the shoulders. I felt my heart surge up into my throat. I was amazed at how little effort it seemed for him to hold me aloft and fling me around. Thank God this was just a playful tussle. He was just overjoyed at the prospect of not losing.

"You see, Jonathan, Mr. Alexandria is a very special man. He makes his living playing chess. He is an international grand master. It is an honour even to be able to play with such a man. Losing to him well is a great accomplishment."

"You don't mind losing?"

"Well, I play to win. But the important thing is to try your hardest, to learn from the match, to gain the respect of your opponent, and to feel that you have grown. Do you understand what I am saying?"

I nodded, although I really wasn't sure what he meant. Losing was losing, winning was winning. It sounded like the sort of thing losers say to make believe they really don't mind losing. What was the point in playing for eighteen years and losing for eighteen years? At some point you should get smart enough to know when to cash your chips in and move to another game. My father was a winner. When he played he won.

"What do you think of the chess set Mr. Alexandria and I play with?" he asked me.

It was a beautiful wooden board. The squares were made from what appeared to be two different types of wood, one dark and the other much lighter. I rubbed my hand across the surface. It was smooth to the touch. I picked up two of the men standing at the side of the board. They were also made of wood. It was obvious they had been handmade.

Each was hand painted with a slightly different expression; some pawns looked scared, some brave, some defiant. I looked at each piece, those off the board as well as those still in play.

"There are only two such boards in the entire world,

Jonathan. The one that sits before you, and its twin, sitting somewhere in the household of Mr. Alexandria. As I made these two sets, I realized that they would be special, and I wanted them to be graced by a genius of the game and not some old Dutch woodworker. I sent Mr. Alexandria the one set, by mail, anonymously, along with my address and my first move. At the end of the game, when I conceded defeat, I thanked him for honouring me with a match. I expected that his obligation was complete, and that I would always have the memory of playing against a grand master. Two weeks later, I received his first move in our next game. During the next few years we have come to know each other. We have become friends. Someday we may even meet."

It was hard to understand how you could be friends with somebody you had never met.

"Finally, Jonathan, I wish to introduce you to my 'baby,' my computer."

"I've never seen a home computer that fancy," I said.

"Even an old man should be allowed an indulgence in his life, and this is mine."

It struck me as strange whenever he called himself an old man. I knew he was probably in his sixties, but he just didn't seem old. Here in his den, describing everything, he sounded like an excited kid. His chess and computer explained his cheers, curses, and mutterings late into the night. He was just having fun.

He went on and on, describing the capabilities of the computer and software and the uses he made of them. With graphics he created landscape designs ("every Dutchman in the world is a landscaper and gardener"), on the word processor he wrote letters and essays for a university course in philosophy ("when you're sixty, the tuition is free"), he played chess against a grand master program, he was learning to improve his French grammar with a language program, he tested his mind against problem-solving software.

And, in an almost guilty manner, he described one further use of the system.

"Jonathan, this must be our little secret," he said in a hushed voice as he motioned for me to come closer. "Do not tell your oma."

I nodded.

"Right now I am spending more and more of my time working on one particular program."

He booted the system, loaded the disk, and waited for the screen to come to life.

Fading from red, the screen swirled to reveal *Glaxatic Adventurers in the Twenty-first Century,* a video game.

"Chess is easy compared with this game. Try as I might, I cannot get any farther than level seven. Have you played this game before, Jonathan?"

In answer, I pushed the enter key to start the game, took the joystick, and proceeded to play. Throughout the game, my grandfather gave me encouragement, cursed the evil enemies who tried to destroy my ships, and cheered on my successes. Finally my last ship was vaporized. Level nine. All that time I'd spent in the video arcades, cutting school, pumping quarters into the machines, had finally come in handy.

"Excellent, Jonathan! You are a grand master Glaxatic Adventurer. I tip my hat to your superior skills and abilities. I hope you feel free to come in here any time. Just as it is an honour to share my chessboard with a master, it is an honour to share this computer with you."

I felt happy. Happier than I could remember since ny father had dropped me off.

Actually, happier than I could remember feeling for long time before I'd been dropped off.

"I've got a deal for you," I tentatively proposed.

"Ah, Jonathan. Always with the deals."

"Well, here's the deal. If you'll teach me how to play hess, I'll teach you how to get to level nine on *Glaxatic dventurers.*"

He smiled and reached out to shake my hand.

"This is a good deal. I accept on one condition. We o not tell your oma anything about the video game art. Besides, this is a good place to play video games. he games and food are free, and you do not have to orry about people bothering you."

My mouth dropped open, and I looked down at the loor. He knew at least about the video arcade.

"Do we have a deal?" he asked.

I reached out to shake his hand.

He took my hand. Instead of shaking it, he pulled ne toward him with amazing power until he had both rms wrapped around me.

"This is an old Dutch custom, and I am an old utchman. We do not just shake hands, we seal the eal with a hug."

I hugged him back.

Twelve

The moment I opened the back door of m
grandparents' home I knew that something wasn
right. It wasn't just that my grandmother wasn't righ
there in the kitchen or that I couldn't hear any sound
but that I couldn't smell supper cooking. I walke
from room to room calling out, "Is anybody home! I
anybody here?" Back in the kitchen I found a not
pinned to the fridge with a large tulip magnet.

Dear Jonathan,

Your opa and I got called out for an emergency. W
will be back later this evening. There is leftover ste
in the fridge. Please help yourself.

Love

Oma

I read the note over twice, folded it in two, and slippe
it into my pocket.

When I lived with my father, I was left on my own
lot. You'd think I'd be used to it by now. I'd almos
always come home from school to an empty house.

Sometimes he'd be home by supper, sometime

later at night, sometimes after I had fallen asleep on the couch with the TV keeping me company. Then I would wake up as he carried me in his arms and put me to bed, still in my clothes. He would lay me down in bed and zip me up in my sleeping bag. I hardly ever had sheets on the bed. I would run my toes along the zipper, feeling the cold metal against my warm foot.

A couple of times my father didn't come home at all. I remember the first time that happened. I woke up, still on the couch, the TV buzzing out a test pattern. I called out for him. There was no answer. I crept up to his room. He wasn't in bed. I looked out the window and saw nothing but the black of night, punctuated by a few scattered stars.

Alone and scared, I went to the kitchen. The clock said it was 3:30 in the morning. When you're alone like that, your head thinks up everything bad that could happen. Your thoughts get wilder and wilder. It gets to the point where you're sure you're going to be murdered by some demented axe-murderer. You just want it to happen quickly so that at least you won't be scared anymore.

I went back to the couch and sat down. I pulled my legs up tight to my chest and wrapped my arms around my legs. I didn't think I'd ever see him again.

Hours later, as the sun was rising, he arrived home. He told me how stupid I had been for worrying, that it was time I grew up, that I wasn't a baby anymore. He was right. I wasn't a baby. I was almost eight years old.

The next time it happened, he was gone for almost three days. I slept on the couch. I made my own meals, making sure I didn't eat too much so there'd be food left for a long time. I went to school and tried to take care of the house. When he finally got back, he didn't explain or apologize. He just said, "See, you did all right."

* * *

I fixed the stew and ate in the kitchen, right out of the pot. No dishes used meant none to wash. I still hated doing dishes.

Every so often I patted the pocket that contained the note. "They'll come back," I said to myself softly. "They'll be back." Before I even realized what I was doing, I found myself checking out the cupboards. There was plenty of food, enough to last for weeks. "Don't be stupid!" I practically yelled to myself. "They'll be back." I patted the note again. "They'll be back."

The ringing of the phone startled me, and I nearly jumped out of my seat. I raced across the room and grabbed it before the first ring had finished echoing off the kitchen cupboards.

"Hello!" I said breathlessly.

"Hello, Jonathan. I'm glad you are home. Did you have supper?"

It was good to hear my grandfather's voice. "Yeah, I did. Will you be home soon?" I tried to hide the sound of worry from my voice. I felt embarrassed.

"Not as soon as I had hoped," he said. "I'm sorry we had to leave you alone without notice."

"That's okay. I'm not a baby anymore," I said, echoing my father's words.

"I know you are not a baby, Jonathan. You are a young man. Still, I would rather have given you an explanation."

I was gripping the phone tightly in my hand. I nodded, as if he could see me through the phone.

"Jonathan, I need you to do something for me."

"Okay, sure. What can I do?"

"Jonathan, in about thirty minutes a man, Mr. Kearns, will be coming to the door. Mr. Kearns used o work for me. I am going to tell you where I keep noney in the house. I want you to go there, count out hree hundred dollars and give it to Mr. Kearns. Can ou do that, Jonathan?"

"Yeah . . . sure."

"Good. Now listen closely. Go into the living room ınd move the green chair. You will find two loose floor oards and a metal bar to pry them up with. Under he boards is a bag containing money. Count out the noney and then replace the boards and push the chair ack into place."

As he spoke I could see the scene in my head.

"Can you do that, Jonathan?"

I nodded.

"Jonathan, can you do that?" He asked again.

"Yes, no problem. Don't worry," I answered.

"Good. He will be there shortly. We will be back efore your bedtime. And, Jonathan . . ." My grandfaher paused.

"Yes?"

"Thank you for your help. I knew I could count on ou. See you soon."

"Okay. Good-bye."

I hung up the phone and went to the living room. The chair was one of those old-fashioned tilt-back ounges. It was covered in green Naugahyde, worn on he arms, and an afghan partially covered it. It looked ıeavy. I pushed against it. Nothing. Then I put my houlder against it and pushed hard. It slowly gave way, nch by inch.

I saw the metal bar right away, but the hardwood floor ooked no different than anyplace else. I looked for the oose boards but couldn't see anything. I knocked gainst them with my knuckles. Two boards made a lifferent sound, more hollow. With my nose practically

at floor level, I could barely see the seams. Then I sa
some faint scratch marks at one end of the neare
board. I picked up the bar, inserted it into the sear
and pried up the first board. The second one easi
followed.

Beneath the missing boards was a cavity about th
size of a toaster. Nestled at the bottom was a larg
pouch. I reached in and pulled it out. It was blac
made of soft leather and closed at the top with a zippe
I undid it and looked in. It was filled with money.

Sitting cross-legged on the floor, I began to pull ou
bills. They were all hundred-dollar bills. I counted o
three and put them aside. I started to close the zippe
but stopped. This money could be the answer to a lot o
my problems. Instead, I began to pull out bills, countin
them and putting them in a pile beside me. Ten . .
twenty . . . forty . . . with many more still inside.

The doorbell rang. My heart raced. It was lik
getting caught with my hand in the cookie jar. I shove
the extra bills back into the pouch and placed it in th
cavity as the bell rang again.

"Hold on. I'm coming," I yelled as I put the boarc
back in place. There wasn't time to put the chair bac
now. I ran to the front door, clutching the thre
hundred dollars tightly in one hand.

I switched on the outside porch light. Through th
window beside the door, I saw a small man standing i
the glow thrown by the bulb. He was about thirty-fiv
or so, small, and wore a worried, beaten-down look.
opened the door.

"Hello. You must be Jonathan," he said.

"That's right," I answered, "and who are you?"

"I'm Mr. Kearns . . . your grandfather called . . .
His voice trailed off, and he looked anxious.

"Yeah, he called. Do you have any ID?" I asked.

"ID?"

"Yeah, you know. Identification, so I can be sure who you are."

He hesitated, like he was confused, but reached into his back pocket and pulled out his wallet. Out of it he produced a driver's licence and handed it to me. The licence identified him as George F. Kearns, and the picture, although bad, was definitely his. I handed him back his ID.

"Thanks. You can't be too careful," I said as I tried to straighten out the crumpled bills before handing them to him.

"Your grandparents told me a lot of very nice things about you, but they didn't tell me how careful you are. It was good to meet you after hearing so much about you."

"Where are my grandparents? What happened?" I had forgotten all about my grandparents.

"They're at my house, or what's left of my house, helping out. We had a fire last night."

"A fire!" I exclaimed.

"Yes. Thank goodness nobody was hurt . . . but we've lost almost everything." His voice trailed off and got sadder sounding. "I only wish I had insurance."

"Will this money help much?" I asked.

"The money's not for the house. Your grandmother was worried about my wife and the baby, so this is to pay for them to go home to her mother's for a few days while we try to make the house livable again. Thank God for your grandparents. Your grandmother has started cleaning and washing, while your grandfather has already drawn up the plans for the new house and is out ordering the wood and supplies I'll need. Those are good people, your grandparents, good people." He paused. "Your grandparents have helped out more people in this town. But enough gabbing, I better be getting back."

Mr. Kearns held out his hand and took mine to shake it. He turned and walked away from the halo cast by our porch light.

I closed the door and went back through the living room. I felt very sorry for Mr. Kearns. It must be a hard thing to lose your home. He was lucky he had people there to help him put it back together. I made sure the floor boards were back in place correctly. Even though I knew the cavity was right there, I couldn't see it. I felt with my fingers and patted the seams. Then, I positioned the chair back over top.

My task finished, I was again alone with my thoughts. "They'll be back. They'll be back soon."

Thirteen

Are you sure you do not wish to join us this evening?" ny grandfather asked after supper the next day.

"No. I've got some homework and things I have to o." I indicated the pile of books on the dining room able.

"Okay. We will be back shortly. If you are hungry, elp yourself to more food. It is good to see you are ating better," my grandmother said.

I waved good-bye and pretended to bury myself in ny extra math homework. The click of the back door nnounced they had left.

I jumped up from the table and ran into the living oom. Then I dropped to my knees, and crawled cross the floor to the window. Parting the curtains ver so slightly, I peaked out and saw their silhouettes valking hand in hand away from the house.

Every night, after dinner was finished and cleaned ip, my grandparents went for a walk. Lately I'd been going with them. Some nights it would be a longer valk, but most evenings it had more to do with talking han walking. We talked together mostly, but with the evening light lasting longer, there were more people trolling themselves. In this town not only did everybody know everybody, but they had known each other orever.

At first I was embarrassed by all the attention sho
ered on me by my grandparents and the people we'
meet. Later, I have to admit, I began to enjoy it.

I got to hear all kinds of stories. Some were abo
the town, other people, my grandparents, and a fe
about my mother. It was a nice kind of strange to he
about her.

I watched my grandparents as they continued t
move away. They got smaller and smaller until the
disappeared. I got up. I did have work to do. Movin
quickly to the green chair, I stopped and studied i
exact position so I could put it back in the same spo
I removed some coins from my pocket and place
four of them, three quarters and a dime, at th
outside edges of the chair's four legs to mark wher
the chair should be returned. Once again I put m
shoulder against the chair and pushed it out of th
way.

This time I found the boards right away. The pouc
was still there. I felt a pang of guilt and removed m
hand from the cavity. Then, I thrust it back in to gra
the pouch.

I unzipped it and took out the bills it containe
counting them one by one and stacking them carefull
on the floor beside me. Total: 257 one hundred-dolla
bills. $25,700. $25,700! I repeated the total over an
over as I fanned myself with the thick wad of money.
peeled two bills from the rest and stuffed them in m
pocket. This was all I needed, right now to get me ou
of trouble.

I knew I still had plenty of time, but I wanted to ge
things back in order. The bills went back into th
pouch, pouch back into the hole, planks in place, an
the chair in its spot. I was about to walk away when
realized I'd left the four markers on the floor. I ben

over and picked them up, placing them into the same pocket as the two hundred dollars.

I went back to the kitchen table to start my math homework. Funny, though, I was having even more trouble than usual. The only numbers I could even think of were two, five, seven, zero, zero.

I now knew not just where, but how much treasure was buried right under my nose. It was reassuring. If anything happened, if I needed a lot of money in a hurry, I knew where to turn.

I wasn't sure what to do now. My father would know what to do. My father. I suddenly realized I had missed a couple of nights, not bothered to look out for his signal. I hadn't even written to him for a while. I scrunched up the aborted math problems I had been working on. I walked over to the sink, opened the cupboard, and tossed the crumpled ball of paper into the garbage can. I returned to the table, took another sheet, and started a letter.

Dear Dad,

I know you must be busy raising the money to come and get me, so I'll keep this letter short. The eight weeks I've been here seem more like three years. It's not that it's bad. They try to treat me okay. It's just that it's boring. Every day is the same. I sleep in the same big bed, go to the same school, talk to the same kids. She's always waiting with a snack when I get home from school. She likes me to call her "Oma" which is Dutch for grandmother. Sometimes I call her that just to make her happy.

I'm doing okay in school. My teacher's name is Roberts. He can be a pain in the butt. There have been a couple of times when I would have liked you around to deal with him, but I guess he's really sor of okay.

There's lots of trouble among the kids in the class. I'm avoiding most of it. Like you always say "when the going gets tough, the smart find an easier way."

Even with all the trouble I've managed to run a scam involving trading cards. All the money tha people have "invested" is coming due soon, so if you don't get here in a couple of weeks, I'll have to think up another angle to sidetrack them. Don't worry though, it won't be hard. Nobody in the whole school seems very bright.

I spend a lot of time in my room. Like I said in my last letter, they don't have a TV, so what am I going to do to entertain myself?

Do you remember those posters I had in my room when we lived in Tupper Lake? I put a couple of them up in my room here. They look pretty coo and give me something to stare at when I'm alone You gave me a couple of them. My favourite is tha picture of the hot-rod Chevy because you said you had one just like it when you were a teenager.

Do you ever miss Tupper Lake? It was the longest we were ever in one place. Do you remember how you'd laugh at me for trying to make supper for you and make the house look tidy? You called me your houseson. I know we had to leave, but it was okay living there.

I still look for your signal every night.

I'll see you soon (I hope),

Jonathan

P.S. I'm doing okay so don't worry about me.

P.P.S. If you came to get me, I could help you get a quick score.

I started to scribble out that last line, thought about it, and left it. I folded the letter and stuffed it in an envelope. I'd mail it tomorrow after school. Maybe I'd drop into the video arcade for a little entertainment.

Fourteen

We had dinner as soon as I got home from school. Tha was strange. I was even more uneasy when my grand father asked me to go for a drive with him. He wa unusually vague when I asked him for more details.

As we drove along, I became more and more ner vous. After about fifteen minutes I felt the truck slow down.

Up ahead I could see a driveway leading to some sort of warehouse. My grandfather turned in, grave and stones shooting off the tires, hitting the undercar riage of the Chevy. Even driving slowly, we lifted a cloud of dust that followed behind and finally over took us as we came to a stop by the building.

It was a long, low structure. One storey, brown aluminum siding, with a few windows up high, one door. Very nondescript. The sort of building you drive by all the time without a second look. I reached for the door handle but was stopped by my grandfather' hand on my shoulder. I turned to face him.

"Jonathan, how much?" he asked.

"How much what?" I asked, my heart doing a flip flop.

"Money. How much money do you owe?"

I was stunned. Obviously he knew something, bu what? "I don't know . . . not much."

This was only half a lie. I owed a fair amount but had no idea just how much. After all, I hadn't intended to pay anybody back so I never kept track. Besides I'd used some of the two hundred dollars to pay back some of the people I'd scammed. But did he know I'd taken that money?

"I want to help you," he said softly.

"You're going to give me money?" I asked hopefully.

"No. But I will help you. Come."

He climbed out of the cab. I followed him toward the building. As we neared, I saw a sign hanging over the entrance.

BEAR WOODWORKING SHOP

I stopped to stare at it. The sign contrasted starkly with the rest of the building. It had vibrant, rich colours and featured a large picture of a bear. This animal looked ferocious with its long bared teeth. It seemed ready to devour anybody who dared to enter the door. Yet, as fierce as it looked, somehow it struck me as familiar and friendly.

"That is an interesting looking bear, eh Jonathan?"

"Yes, sir. It looks . . . I don't know . . . kind of like I know that bear from somewhere."

My grandfather walked over and stood directly beneath the sign. He turned and imitated the posture and fierce gesture of the creature. It was then that I realized that the bear on the sign was my "bear" of a grandfather. His snarl dissolved into an embarrassed smile, and then he laughed.

"Maybe you think I am a silly old fool, but this is, I should say, was, my shop. Your mama painted that sign for me over twenty years ago. I sold the shop almost six years ago, but they still keep the name and the sign.

It is a good name. People respect the quality of the work we did over the years."

All at once he grabbed me and lifted me off my feet, holding me in a gentle but powerful bear hug and then lifting me higher so that I sat in his arms.

"I may be an old bear, but I am still a bear," he growled. "Come along my little cub. I want to show you my shop. As well I want to show them my Jonathan."

I knew that at my age I was too old to be carried around, but somehow it felt okay with him. Maybe because he was so big. Even if I didn't understand why, it still felt good.

He put me down but kept his arm around my shoulder as we came to the big door. He slid it open, and we were instantly swallowed by the wave of sound that came pouring out. We waded into the building.

It was huge and filled with gigantic lathes, routers, sanders, drill presses, band saws, rippers, and circular saws. They were just larger versions of the machines that lived in our garage, and I knew what most of them could do. Since building my bed together, my grandfather and I had worked on different projects. He was always right there, watching over me, but let me do most of the work myself. He was good like that.

Each piece of equipment in the shop screamed out its own particular song as machine and wood came together. I could taste the sawdust in my mouth. It floated around, suspended in the air, until it settled onto the floor or machines. There was a heavy coating everywhere, which seemed so strange, so different from our sparkling clean workshop. I thought this was disrespectful to the machines.

My grandfather bent over and cupped his hands over my ear. "This is like the sound of beautiful music to me. Oma thinks that working with noisy machines all these years has made me a little deaf. I can hear okay, but sometimes it is easier to just let her think what she wants and I get a little peace. But do not go telling her this. It must be another of our little secrets."

As he was talking, the noise around us diminished and then faded away almost completely, except for the gentle humming of what sounded like a hive of vacuum cleaners.

We were rushed on all sides by the men who had turned off their machines. With smiling faces and outstretched hands they yelled out shouts of greetings. They spoke in different languages, and my grandfather would answer each in the language he had been addressed. I learned that he spoke not just Dutch and English, but also Portuguese, Italian, and Spanish, too. He took time to introduce me to each man. I recognized Mr. Kearns as he came over to offer his greetings. They all shook my hand or slapped me on the back.

I saw him at the same moment I heard him. He was half bald, with shirt sleeves rolled up, a tie hanging loosely around his neck, a scowl on his face, and he was yelling as he came in our direction.

"All right, you guys. Everybody get back to work. Everybody get back to . . ." He stopped mid-sentence, and his face seemed to brighten. "Herbie! Herbie. Just the man I wanted to see."

"Herbie?" I thought. I could see my grandfather being called a lot of different things, but Herbie was definitely not one of them.

The man moved through the crowd that had gathered around us and then bumped me out of the way. He grabbed my grandfather's hand and pumped it vigorously.

"Herbie, I need you for an important job. We're stuck." He sounded like a machine gun.

"Hello, Frank, and how are you today?"

"Fine, fine, fine. Now I've got a job we're stuck on," he continued.

"Frank, this is my grandson, Jonathan. You probably didn't notice him because you are standing on top of him."

"We've had problems with the design specifications for the new order and we're way behind schedule," he replied, completely ignoring both me and what my grandfather had said.

"Frank," my grandfather started again.

"No matter what we try, it just doesn't come out right."

"Frank," he said slightly louder.

"The whole order's backed up, I don't know what we're going to do."

"Frank!" he practically yelled.

"Yeah, Herbie?"

"Frank, this is my grandson, Jonathan," he said as he reached over and grabbed my arm to pull me to his side.

There was a blank look on Frank's face. He looked at my grandfather, looked at me, at my grandfather again, and then finally back to me. A smile grew on his face.

"No kidding?" asked Frank.

"Frank, would I kid you?" All around us, the crowd of men started chuckling and exchanging looks at the thought of my grandfather kidding Frank.

"Well, good to meet ya, kid. Anyway, we've got real problems here, Herbie. I need to talk to you."

"Okay, Frank. We can talk." My grandfather turned to me. "Each machine is surrounded by a yellow line. Look at anything, but do not go inside those lines."

He turned to Frank. "It certainly is messy around

here, lots of scraps of wood lying around and sawdust everywhere."

"Yeah, you know how hard it is to get help to do that sort of thing."

"All right, Frank. Let us go back to your office, so you can loosen your tie even more. Then we'll solve your problems and get your blood pressure lower."

"Great! Great! Now everybody get back to work. We're behind schedule already," he shouted over his shoulder as they started to walk away.

The men drifted back to their jobs. The noise level rose as each machine came to life. It was exciting as I wandered around watching the men work. Some of them took a few seconds to talk to me over the deafening noise. Others gestured and smiled. Mr. Kearns, a big smile on his face, reached into his pocket and produced a chocolate bar that he waved in the air. He took the bar and threw it in my direction. It dropped just in front of me, skidded along the floor between my legs, and came to rest in a pile of sawdust. I ran after it, dusted it off on my shirt, ripped it open, and took a big bite.

At the far end of the shop, behind a glass-fronted office, I could see my grandfather and Frank standing before a drafting table, talking. As I watched, they stopped their discussion and re-emerged onto the shop floor.

Frank had a big smile on his face and moved his arms all over the place excitedly. A little more coordination to that movement and I thought he might just get airborne.

Then Frank rushed up to me, grabbed my hand, shook it, and yelled out a speech. Over the din of the machines all I could make out was "congratulations . . . hard work . . . next week."

I nodded, shook his hand back, and smiled. Frank let go of my hand, gave my grandfather a big hug, and walked away.

My grandfather then went to each man and shook hands. We moved to the exit, and as the door slid shut behind us, the noise was shut off. Still, I could hear the machines buzzing in my ears. I stuck a finger in one ear to try to shake loose the sound.

"Your ears are ringing?" asked my grandfather.

"A little bit. Nothing too bad," I answered.

"Next week, you will wear ear protection."

"Next week?" I asked.

"Yes, when you start your part-time job."

"Part-time job? What part-time job?"

He smiled. "I told Frank that I could not help solve his design problems in such a messy shop, and that I knew a hard and trustworthy worker who could take care of the mess. You are a hard worker. You are trustworthy. You do want the job, do you not?"

"Yeah, I guess I do. Will you be around?" I asked hesitantly.

"At first. It will probably take me a week or more to redesign this order. After that, you will be there without me. I know that you will do a good job," he said. "Jonathan, I got you the job. What you do now, how you work and what you do with the money you earn, is up to you."

We climbed into the truck and started to drive away. I chuckled. My grandfather looked at me out of the corner of his eye.

"There is something funny, Jonathan?"

"Oh, nothing. Nothing at all . . . Herbie."

We both laughed together.

Fifteen

"Jonathan, slow down and chew your breakfast slowly," pleaded my grandmother. "The boys have not even arrived yet, so they will not leave without you."

"I'm not rushing that much," I mumbled in protest. Then I realized my mouth was full of pancake, sausage, cereal, and juice. I chewed hard and took a humongous swallow. "Okay, maybe a little slower."

She buzzed around the kitchen, singing softly and humming as she cooked and cleaned dishes. The late February sun had just peeked over the horizon. The little light that came through the kitchen window was filtered through the giant evergreen trees that hung over the house like gigantic umbrellas. The wood stove, in the corner of the kitchen, crackled and radiated warmth throughout the room. It felt nice just to be here.

"Where's Grandfather? It's not like him to miss breakfast . . . or any other meal," I said jokingly.

"He will be in shortly. He is just doing some packing," she answered.

"Packing? Is he running away from home?" I asked as I cleaned the last scrape of pancake from my plate.

My grandmother turned from the stove, balancing a pile of pancakes on a spatula. Without missing a beat she placed them on my plate.

"And do not even dare tell me that you are too full or do not have enough time. Eat! It is cold up there and this will pad your tummy a little. As it is, people must think I am a poor cook or do not feed you. Such a bag of bones you are."

I was learning that there wasn't much sense in arguing with her, so I shovelled in a big mouthful. I had already put on more than a few pounds since I had arrived.

My grandfather came in through the back door, a gust of cold, crisp air pushing in behind him.

"Good morning, my grandson. I have finished packing a knapsack for you. Did you leave me any hotcakes?"

"Why?" I asked playfully. "You don't need any more padding."

My grandmother chuckled as she put a giant plate of pancakes on my grandfather's plate. He took his seat.

"What did you pack?" I asked.

"All kinds of things you will need, or may need," he answered with his mouth full of breakfast.

"Herbert!" my grandmother yelled as she flicked him on the back of the head with a tea towel. "Such manners! Swallow your food before you talk. You are worse than a little child."

He swallowed before continuing. He knew even better than me that it was not wise to argue. "I put in an extra woolen sweater, an old felt hat, two extra pairs of gloves, a towel, sandwiches, an extra puck, and a big thermos filled with soup. I put your skates inside as well. I have looped the whole bag over the end of your hockey stick."

"I'm only going for the morning, not for a vacation you know."

"I just wanted to make sure you would have everything you needed to have a good time with your friends," he answered. "I hope the skates will fit. They are old but Mr. Johanssen down the street said they are still good. He was pleased you could make use of his son's old skates."

The conversation was broken off by a thundering knock on the kitchen door. I jumped up to get my coat, while my grandmother ran to open the door.

"Good morning, Mr. and Mrs. van Gees," came a chorus from Tommy, Vern, and Stan as they were ushered into the kitchen.

By the time I was back with my coat, my grandfather was lecturing them about the ice and safety and being careful. I heard them repeatedly answer "Yes, Sir" or "No, Sir" in response to his words.

"Now," my grandfather added, "since you have all listened so carefully I will give you a lift. It is at least a fifty-minute walk. Better you should save your time and legs for hockey instead of for walking. Here, Jonathan, take my keys and start the truck to get it warmed up. Scrape off the ice from the windshield. I will be out as soon as I finish my breakfast."

We all thanked him as we grabbed our bags and ran out to the truck.

***

Soon we were all sitting in the back of the truck, tucked in behind the cab, with the cold air streaming over our heads. We drove past the school, beyond the last subdivision, to an old, deserted farm. It had acres and acres of fields, a forest, a big pond, a stream, and the abandoned farm buildings.

The truck slowed down and pulled slightly off the

road. The plows, in clearing the road throughout the winter, had created giant piles of snow, twice as high as the cab of the truck, that closed the road in on both sides. We jumped off the back and waved good-bye as he pulled away.

My grandfather stopped just ahead, where the distance between the walls of snow was slightly wider. We climbed the snowbank, and while the other three slid down the far side, I watched as he jiggled the truck back and forth to turn it around. He drove past and honked and we waved to each other. I watched as the truck disappeared down the road.

Quickly I slid down the embankment to catch up to my friends. There was a well-worn path through the snow, beaten down by the feet of skaters who had walked this way on other days. On this morning though, we were the first to come. There were no prints in the fresh dusting of snow that had fallen that night.

"We'll have the whole pond to ourselves!" yelled Stan as he ran ahead and we ran to catch him.

The pond was covered by smooth, clear ice. The wind had blown the snow into soft drifts at the far end. The pond looked like an immense bed with the covers kicked off and clinging to the bottom.

While I was gazing at the scenery, Stan and Tommy had plopped to the ice and were pulling on their skates. I sat down, anxiously pulled off my boots, and started lacing up my skates. It had been a long time, since that winter in Tupper Lake, that I had spent any time on skates.

Soon, we were gliding across the surface, the skates leaving scratch marks on the mirror of ice. The air was filled with the shshing of blades, punctuated by the whack of pucks against sticks.

After the initial rush of activity we stopped and drew deep breaths. The sun was rising higher, and the sky was blue and cloudless. The air already felt warmer against my face. The trees that surrounded the pond shielded us from the wind. In the excitement of the moment I hadn't noticed at first that Vern wasn't with us.

"Where's Vern?" I asked.

Tommy motioned over his shoulder. "He's taking care of business."

I looked past Tommy. There was smoke coming from the chimney of a little shack poking out of the snow on the far side of the pond.

"That's the old smokehouse," continued Tommy. "Vern has the fire going. He'll probably heat up some hot chocolate after our game."

"You know Vern," added Stan. "My father says he's the sort of guy who, if you give him a sheep, will give you back mutton stew, lamb chops, and a knitted wool suit and socks."

At that moment Vern came skating across the pond. As he skated, he smacked his stick against the ice every few strides. The sound reverberated off the surrounding trees and echoed back from all sides.

"Did you hear the sound?" he asked as if he were discussing a science experiment. "The ice gets thicker over here. The closer you get to the open water by the spring, the thinner it gets."

"Is it dangerous?" I asked, concerned. My only skating had been in indoor rinks. You couldn't fall through the ice in an arena, but even if you could, it was only five centimetres to the painted pavement below.

"Nah, no worry. The pond is only about a metre deep. The worst you'll get is soaked," said Vern.

"It never freezes over there because the spring that feeds the pond is warm," Tommy added.

"And if you do fall in, you can just go into the smokeshack." Vern nodded toward the hut.

"Yeah," continued Stan, "Vern will dry, mend, and press your pants while he feeds you tea with honey and freshly baked muffins. You are baking muffins in there aren't you, Vernie?"

"Even if I was, you wouldn't be getting any," answered Vern as he used his stick to hook Stan's skates, sending him crashing to the ice like a sack of potatoes.

Almost instantaneously, Stan bounced back up and, cursing as he went, chased Vern across the pond.

"I guess that means you and me stand the two of them," said Tommy as he smacked me on the butt with the blade of his stick.

* * *

Two hours later we sat together in the smokeshack. The game was over. The final score was 197 to 196. Or something like that. Both sides claimed victory. Our coats and mitts and hats were hanging from the hooks strung across the ceiling of the small, squat building. Before the farm had been deserted, these hooks would have held sides of meat, slowly being cured.

Our clothes were soaked, both from our sweat and from falling on the ice, where puddles had begun to form. The sun had warmed the air, and it felt like the beginning of spring.

We gorged down sandwiches and soup and the hot chocolate that Vern heated up for us.

I was grateful for the big lunch my grandfather had packed. With each course of our meal, we stripped off nother layer of soggy clothes, the pile rising as the emperature inside the shack rose.

Finally, Tommy and I were just in our pants, Vern n undershirt and pants, and Stan just in his Skivvies. We all stood up and started singing and pretending to play guitar. We broke up laughing when Stan said we ooked like a bad rock video. Standing there, singing n his underwear, Stan looked like an extra in a Madonna tape.

Stan sat down. "Do you guys know what would really hit the spot right now?" he asked.

"A homemade muffin and a cup of tea with honey?" oked Vern.

"Well, yeah, that would be nice, Vernie, but what I was really thinking about was a swim," he answered.

"A swim?" we all echoed in unison.

"Yeah," he continued, "a nice, cool, refreshing swim. Doesn't that sound good, guys?"

"A nice swim," said Tommy, nodding. "A nice cool swim, like a polar-bear dip." He rose to his feet and started to undo his pants.

"Come on, guys," implored Vern. "Quit kidding around. Even by the spring the water is still almost freezing."

Tommy started to chant, "Swim, swim, swim," and Stan quickly joined in.

"Can't I talk you guys out of this?" asked Vern with obvious concern in his voice.

But they just kept on with their chorus, "Swim, swim, SWIM, SWIM," getting louder and faster.

"I guess not," Vern's mouth seemed to say, as he couldn't make himself heard over their increasingly loud voices. Vern rose from his seat by the fire, pulled his shirt over his head, and joined in. Within seconds

all three were standing by the door, dressed in onl
their underwear.

"Well, Jonathan?" asked Tommy.

I still wasn't even completely sure what they meant
My mouth was hanging open and I just sat staring a
them, dumbstruck. Tommy shrugged and turne
around as all three stripped out of their undergar
ments. Three white bottoms, practically glowing in th
dim light of the shack, ran through the door. Th
door, attached to a spring, slammed and the shack wa
suddenly silent.

I heard them shriek as they ran across the snow
then a splash as they hit the water, followed instantl
by an even bigger scream.

In half a second, I had made my decision. I sprinte
after them, one leg out of my pants before I had even
hit the door. Hopping, running, tugging off the othe
leg, I ran, fell, got up, and kicked my pants off just a
I reached the edge of the opening. I wiggled out of m
underwear as the other three stood waist deep in th
water, cheering me on.

"Way to go, Jonathan. Now jump in, quick!" yelle
Vern.

"Is it cold?" I asked through chattering teeth.

"Of course it's cold, you idiot," Tommy answered.

"But quick, quick. Jump in, quick," begged Vern.

"Or else," giggled Stan as he lowered himself down
farther into the water, "turn around and wave to Stac
and her friends."

I chuckled. "Give me a break, Stan. Do you think
I'm really dumb enough to fall for that?"

All three smiled and ducked lower in the water unti
their whole bodies were submerged except for thei
heads.

The voice that came from behind me sent a shiver up my spine that had nothing to do with the cold.

"Hi, Jonathan. . . . It's good to . . . see you," Stacy's voice rang out to an accompaniment of giggles.

I dove headfirst into the water, and tried to stay under as long as I could. I surfaced to see the girls skating away to the far end of the pond. We pulled ourselves out of the icy water and ran for the shack as if our lives depended upon it.

Sixteen

"Hi guys," Stacy said as she and Jennifer stopped in front of the table where we sat eating our lunches.

Vern, Stan, Tommy, and I all mumbled "Hello" as we wiped sandwich crumbs from our faces. It had been a few weeks since we were discovered skinny-dipping at the pond. I could now face her without going completely red in the face.

The two girls stood there smiling nervously and shifting from foot to foot.

"Go ahead," said Jennifer as she elbowed Stacy in the side.

Stacy shot her a dirty look but quickly turned back to us with a smile on her face. A smile, I might add, that was nothing short of wonderful.

"It's my birthday next week," she started, "and my parents said that I could have a party at our house. I was hoping that you guys could come. I'm inviting everybody in the whole class."

"Wow, that sounds like fun," said Tommy.

"You must have some big place to have the whole class come over," Stan said.

"It's not that big." Jennifer sounded defensive. "I think it's just about the same size as my house."

"Maybe not big in the Heights," Vern added, "but compared to the houses in town it must be massive."

"Anyway, now that we know where, when is it going to be?" Tommy asked.

"This Saturday, around 4:00," Stacy responded.

"That means we can't go, Stan," said Tommy.

"Yeah," confirmed Stan. "Tommy and me will be away all weekend at my uncle's cottage. We're helping him to open it up. You know, put in the dock, clean up the property, open the windows, and things like that. Maybe we'll do a little fishing or hunting even."

"Hunting? Come on, Stan, the closest your uncle ever let you get to a gun was last year when he told you to shut up and go to sleep or he'd shoot you," Tommy joked.

"I hope you both have fun at the cottage. It's too bad you can't make it," Stacy said. Jennifer nodded.

"But, you two can make it, can't you?" She turned her full attention to Vern and I.

Vern shook his head. "Better count me out. I work with my dad on Saturdays. This is his busiest time of year. I'll be around the Heights but not at your party."

"Couldn't you ask him for the day off?" Jennifer asked.

"I could, and I know he'd give it to me . . . but . . . he needs my help. It's my job."

Both girls now focused exclusively on me. Stacy gave me a big smile. She had nice teeth. A lot of nice teeth. I felt my feet start to melt under her gaze.

"You can come, can't you, Jonathan?" Stacy pleaded.

"You don't have to work or anything, do you?" added Jennifer.

My tongue didn't seem to want to answer. My father was a master at speaking to females and always seemed to know just what to say. Me, I seemed to lose the ability to speak English. Finally I was able to croak out an answer.

"No, I'm off work by 12:00 on Saturdays."

"Then you can come!" Stacy said excitedly.

"I guess so," I mumbled through my thick tongue.

"There'll be lots of food," Jennifer said.

"Food," I echoed.

"And games," said Stacy.

"Games," I mumbled.

"And music," Jennifer noted.

"Music," I repeated.

"And dancing," they both giggled and looked toward each other.

"I'm sorry you all can't come . . . but I'm happy you can, Jonathan," Stacy said, flashing me another of those wonderful smiles.

I wanted to say something witty or bright. But "Yeah" was all that came out of my mouth.

"Okay, we better get going. You four were the first people we invited, so we have to talk to everybody else," said Jennifer as she grabbed Stacy by the arm and led her away. We all grunted good-bye.

We picked up our sandwiches and went back to the task at hand, cramming down our lunches before the bell went.

A tremendous burp suddenly erupted from Stan's lips and we all broke up laughing. Stacy and Jennifer, who were now talking to another table of kids from our class, turned around and looked at us. They probably thought we were laughing at them.

"It was hard to hold that in. I almost belched in the middle of Stacy batting her eyes at Jonathan."

"At me?" I asked incredulously.

"Yeah, at you," Tommy answered.

"We all know you like her," added Vern.

"And it looks like she likes you," finished Stan.

I took a long drink from my milk. I hadn't been aware I was that obvious. I did like Stacy.

It wasn't just that Stacy was really good-looking. It was more the way she was. She was probably the smartest person in the class, but she never showed people up. She was from the Heights but treated everybody, even the townies, the same way. I liked her because she was kind. That, and the days she wore her soft pink sweater and gave me that smile. Wow.

Tommy broke me from my daydream. "It just doesn't figure," he said with that playful tone in his voice I had come to know so well. "There's four guys at this table and you're, at best, the fourth best-looking, so why would Stacy like you?"

Stan rolled his eyes back, grabbed both his ears, stretching them out like Dumbo, and opened his mouth to reveal a partially chewed peanut butter and jelly sandwich.

"Okay," noted Tommy, "the third best-looking guy at this table."

"I know what it is about Jonathan," Stan mumbled as he swallowed his mouthful of lunch. "She likes birds."

"Birds?" I repeated.

"Parrots," he replied.

"Parrots?" I echoed.

"See what I mean," said Stan. Then, accompanied by Vern and Tommy, he broke into gales of laughter.

"Oh, Jonathan, my darling," began Stan in his best attempt to mimic a girl's voice, "there will be food."

"Food," answered Tommy, trying to sound like a parrot.

"And music," added Stan, in a half-decent imitation of Stacy's voice.

"Squawk, music," repeated Tommy.

"And dancing," giggled both Stan and Vern as they rose from their seats and began to waltz around the table.

"Squawk, dancing. Squawk, dancing. Jonathan want a cracker. Jonathan want a cracker," continued Tommy.

Mercifully, the lunch bell sounded. We all gathered our stuff. I grabbed my things and moved away from the table first, with the three of them following close on my heels. As we moved through the crowd, the three of them continued to do their best to sound like parrots. It wasn't just my imagination that we were gathering a lot of attention as we shuffled between the other kids moving toward the exit.

Just through the lunchroom doors, I realized I didn't have my math book.

"I've got to go back. I forgot something."

"Squawk, we'll see you in class," replied Tommy.

"Yeah, squawk. See you in class, darling, squawk," added Stan.

I pushed against the current of kids hustling out through the doors on their way to class. I felt like my feet were just barely touching the ground. I had this happy feeling inside that was leaking out through the silly grin I knew was on my face.

Stacy liked me. I sort of had it figured out. I'd seen enough of my father's girlfriends and the way they acted around him. There was a warm, fuzzy, buzzing that came from the back of my head, I felt so happy. Too happy to see anything as I bent down to get my book where it had fallen under the table.

A foot hit me in the back, and I was knocked sprawling onto the floor. I instantly tried to get back to my feet but was stopped by a warning.

"Don't try to get up," snarled Alexander.

"Stay down there," threatened Justin.

I stayed where I was, stretched out on the floor, partially underneath the table, with the two of them standing right over me. The lunchroom was almost empty and all the supervisors gone. I could hear there were still a few kids at the far end of the room, trying to get out. But, from underneath the table there was no way I could see them and no way they could see me.

"We're really worried about your health, townie," said Alexander in a sick, sweet voice.

"We rushed right over to see if you were okay when we saw you had fallen down.' Now we're right up close, we can see you don't look too good. Maybe you're coming down with something," continued Justin.

"That's it," added Alexander. "The townie is coming down with something, some sort of townie disease. You better go home and take it easy, you know. Like lie down all day Saturday or you might get hurt . . . I mean sicker."

"Or even deader." It was Justin again. "We wouldn't want you to infect the other people at that party on Saturday. We don't want any townie diseases up there. You understand what I'm saying?"

I rolled over and stared up at them numbly. Jason put the toe of his shoe against my chest. "You do understand?"

"You better listen to Dr. Alexander, townie," warned Justin as both chuckled at his little joke.

I looked up at them looking down at me and nodded.

"That's good. See, he isn't really that stupid after all. Matter of fact he's starting to look healthier already. And remember, if you want to stay healthy, don't go butting into places where you don't belong," threatened Alexander.

"Besides, townie, we want you to stay healthy. We're protecting our investment. After all, you owe us a lot of money," said Justin, his lip curled up in a snarl.

I didn't know what he meant. There were a lot of kids who I had either borrowed money from or had "invested" in my trading-card scam, but I wasn't stupid enough to do either of those things with those two.

"Some of the kids you owed money to figured they'd never see it again. So we paid them to take over your debts. We knew we'd have no trouble making you pay up. So now you owe us big time," said Alexander, chuckling.

"Yeah, big time. Now stay down there on the floor where you belong until we're gone," added Justin. He gave me a look of total disgust. It was the sort of expression normally reserved for something you found stuck underneath your chair. They turned and walked away, laughing.

Just before they got to the door, Alexander spun around and yelled across the room. "And don't get any ideas about telling Kraemer or anybody else about this conversation or you'll get real sick real fast."

In a few seconds they were gone, and the doors swung shut behind them. The room was silent except for the sound my heart was making. How could I tell anybody, especially Tommy? How do you tell people what a coward you are? Anyway, it was just some stupid party. It wasn't worth getting beaten up over a dumb thing like that. Besides, I didn't like Stacy that much.

My dad always said to stay out of things, to not get involved. Anyway, I'd probably be gone soon.

Seventeen

"Okay, boys. That wraps it up for now. Enjoy the rest of your lunch hour," said Mr. Roberts.

Tommy and I closed our books, got up from our seats, and walked over to grab our lunch bags from our hooks. We lingered at the door to the hall.

Mr. Roberts looked up from the papers he was marking. "You two had better get going if you hope to eat."

"But, you didn't give us any extra homework," said Tommy.

"No, I didn't. The two of you did good work today. You understand the concept so well I don't feel you need any extra work. Do you want some homework?"

"NO!" we yelled out in unison.

"Because I wouldn't want to disappoint you boys. If you wait a minute, I can probably find some."

"No, thanks. That's okay, sir," I replied.

"But I wouldn't want to break a good habit," he said.

"That's okay, thanks. We better get going for lunch," Tommy insisted. We bumped into each other trying to get out the door, fast.

"Boys!" we heard Mr. Roberts yell. "Are you sure you don't want any homework?"

As we raced down the hall, his voice was quickly drowned out by the noise of other kids talking, laughing, and yelling in the lunchroom. We moved through the crowded room to join Vern and Stan, who were just finishing their lunches.

"Wow!" said Tommy, laughing. "What did you guys do? Suck down your food without chewing?"

"Yeah, and now we're going to hose down yours," Stan answered as he grabbed the Twinkie Tommy had just taken out of his bag. He tried to stuff it into his mouth, wrapper and all. Tommy quickly reached out, and they struggled over it until the squished treat popped out of the wrapper and plopped onto the floor. Our laughter and play stopped when we looked up to see Justin, Alexander, Shaun, and the rest of their buddies standing at the end of our table.

"You guys are such dorks you don't even know how to eat like humans," scowled Justin.

Alexander cleared his throat. He often did that before he started talking, like maybe it would get his mind unstuck. Fat chance. He started to talk.

"I've got a riddle for you jerks. It involves math, so I know Tommy and Jonathan won't get it."

"So what's the riddle?" egged on Justin.

"What do you get when you add one stupid townie who doesn't know how to add with another stupid townie who doesn't know how to multiply?"

"I give up. What do you get?" asked Shaun.

"The answer is half the people sitting at this table," said Alexander, accompanied by the snorting and chuckling from the rest of the hyenas.

Tommy very, very slowly put down the sandwich he had started munching and turned his gaze upon them. I held my breath and waited for the explosion that was sure to follow. Tommy had a confused look on his face.

"I don't get it," he said as he picked up his sandwich again and took a big bite.

Alexander looked even more confused than Tommy had. He and his friends mumbled to each other, then moved away as if they had been dismissed.

Tommy scooped up the smushed Twinkie from the floor. "I just can't stand to see good food go to waste," he said, pitching it across the room and hitting Justin squarely on the back of the head.

That's when all hell broke loose.

"FOOD FIGHT!" people yelled from all four corners of the lunchroom. Before the words could even fade away, a barrage of edible ammunition started to fly.

The few late arrivals, like Tommy and me, had lots of food to fight with. Stan and Vern, their lunches already eaten, started to heave pieces of ours.

Apples, oranges, and half-eaten peanut butter and jelly sandwiches careened across the room. Cartons of milk spewed out liquid as they spun through the air, juice boxes hit the walls and exploded. Lunch bags filled with garbage, and an occasional book with pages cartwheeling open, flew above our heads. And the noise — kids screaming, laughing, calling, cursing, the solid crunch of an apple hitting something hard, chair and table legs screeching across the floor, kids grunting as they tossed their food with all their might. The lunchroom supervisors stood at the centre of the room, arms outstretched, their yells not audible over the other sounds, being totally ignored. Kids ducked beneath tables, hiding from flying food while throwing recycled lunch fragments that had hit them or landed nearby. Chairs were used as shields. A couple of kids jumped onto tables and dared anybody to hit them before being driven back down by an avalanche of food. There was a scramble of students out of the lunchroom, with or without their bags and books.

Suddenly the lights went out for a couple of seconds and then flicked back on.

"Everybody sit down. Everybody stop immediately!" yelled Mrs. Volley, our principal. She was flanked by half a dozen teachers who had emptied out of the staffroom and were now fanning out across the lunchroom.

Dead silence. Kids caught standing on tabletops with arms back, suspended in mid-throw, quickly climbed down and tried to melt into the floor.

"All right!" she yelled again. This time her voice echoed off the silence of the room. She lowered her voice to a loud speaking level. "Everybody go back to your classes. Let's start with the back tables. Walking. Back to your class." She gave each of us a good look as we filed past. My stomach was growling, partly because I hadn't eaten anything and partly because I knew we hadn't heard the last of this.

"Too bad we didn't get there five minutes later. We wouldn't have been involved in any of this," I whispered to Tommy as we moved down the hall.

Tommy gave me a strange look. "Jonathan, we weren't just involved in it, we started it. Remember?"

Halfway back to class the bell sounded, ending lunch twenty minutes early. Soon after we took our seats in silence, we heard the crackle of the intercom as it came to life. There was the sound of somebody blowing into the microphone.

"May I have your attention, please." It was our vice-principal, Mr. Tom (The Terminator) Turner. The voice of doom. "As most of you are well aware, there was an altercation in the lunchroom this afternoon." He cleared his throat. "I want all those who are responsible to come down to the office immediately." There was a slight pause. "And if those involved do not come forward to take responsibility, then all students who eat in the lunchroom, whether they took part or not, will be punished."

There was a collective groan from our class, and probably throughout the whole school. A couple of kids muttered something about it not being fair.

Mr. Roberts stood up, raised his arms, and gave us his famous look, the one that could peel paint. Everybody was smart enough to shut up instantly.

"That is all," were the final words spoken by Mr. Turner as the intercom stopped buzzing.

Mr. Roberts sat down at his desk. The room was so quiet I could hear the seat of his pants hit the seat of his chair. Tommy rose from his chair and started walking toward the door.

"Tommy?" asked Mr. Roberts.

Tommy kept on walking. "I've got an appointment with The Terminator, I mean Mr. Turner. Don't wait up for me. I could be a while."

The door clanged shut behind him. The kids quietly mumbled to each other. I looked around and knew what I needed to do. I took a deep breath and then pushed against my desk with both arms. My legs felt wobbly as I took to my feet and started toward the door.

"Jonathan?" asked Mr. Roberts, his voice incredulous. "You, too?"

Following Tommy's example, I kept walking. "I don't want Tommy to get lonely. I'll be back later . . . I hope."

Once in the hall I ran and caught Tommy just before he got to the office. He flashed me a quick smile. Then our faces took on a serious look to face The Terminator.

* * *

From the lunchroom, later that afternoon, we heard the announcement.

"May I have your attention, please. Those responsible for the incident in the lunchroom today have come forward. There will be no further consequences for other students. That is all."

Through the closed doors we could hear faint cheers escape from classrooms and rumble down the corridor.

Down on my knees, rag in hand, bucket by my side, I said to Tommy, "Great news, huh? Nobody will be punished."

Tommy stopped washing and sat up on his haunches. "Jonathan."

"Yeah?"

"Shut up." His words were instantly followed by a wet rag that bounced off the top of my head. I turned around to see him give me one of his patented goofy smiles.

* * *

Four hours later, the job was almost completed. My knees were sore and my hands red and wrinkled. The door opened, and Mr. Roberts walked in across our clean and washed floor. We stopped working to watch him as he strolled around the room, inspecting the walls, floor, tables, and chairs.

He let out a long, low whistle and then spoke. "I

don't think I've ever seen this room look so clean. It practically sparkles."

"Gee thanks," grunted Tommy.

He walked toward us. "Maybe you two could get into trouble every couple of days and we could lay off the cleaning staff," he said, chuckling. "How are you boys feeling?"

"Sore," I answered.

"Tired," replied Tommy.

Mr. Roberts sat down on one of the newly washed tables. He quickly got up and looked at the back of his pants. He made a face that showed total disgust. As he turned around, it was hard not to notice that it looked like he had wet himself.

"I'm too old to wet my pants," he said, shaking his head. "Anyway, I just came from seeing Mr. Turner. Would you like to know what he said?"

Our ears perked up, but our spirits remained low as we waited for the next punishment.

"He said that, if you were finished in here, it was up to me to think of other punishments and to have a word with both of you. It looks to me as if this job is completed. As for other punishments," he paused for what was only a few seconds but seemed like forever, "I think you two have been punished enough."

We both stood up, trying to get the kinks out of our backs.

"Hold it. I'm not through with you two yet. Mr. Turner said I was to have a word with you. Come over here. Have a seat, and try not to sit on a wet spot."

We abandoned our buckets, walked stiffly over, and sat down.

"The word I want to say to you both is, 'proud.'"

I could see Tommy was as lost as I was.

"Boys, try not to look like two confused baboons. Close your mouths, and I'll explain. There were probably two hundred students who had a part in making this mess, even if you two did start it. Nobody else accepted any responsibility. So," he concluded, "I'm proud of you both."

I still felt a little confused but mostly relieved.

"Now, get going. Go home. I'll put away your mops and buckets. Get going," he ordered.

Just as the doors to the lunchroom were closing behind us, we heard Mr. Roberts yell out, "Boys, are you sure you don't want any extra homework?" followed by his loud laughter.

We scrambled down the hall, fast, walking but not running.

Eighteen

It seemed like hours since I had gone to bed. I tossed and turned, kicked the sheets off, punched and repositioned the pillows, but nothing worked. I couldn't get to sleep. Maybe I needed sleep, but I needed to talk even more.

I got out of bed and turned on the light. The light dribbled out of the room, and I followed the trail along the hall and down the stairs. It led me to the door of the den. Light glowed from the crack underneath the closed door. I knocked once and walked in.

Opa was seated on the floor, looking eye level at his handmade chess set, in such concentration he didn't hear me enter. He sat motionless, as if he were in a trance. I cleared my throat. He glanced up, but there was no look of surprise at my late night appearance. He gestured for me to come over.

I joined him on the floor and stared at the pieces. Most of the white pieces, those being played by my opa, sat beside the board. The few white pieces still in play were hopelessly outnumbered by black ones. It looked like time to concede.

Finally, he spoke. "I'm afraid to take my eyes off the board. Maybe the move might go away. Do you see it?"

All I saw was White going down to another defeat.

Mr. Alexandria, playing black, had turned what had earlier looked like a draw into another loss for Opa.

"No," I answered, "I don't see anything . . . yet."

Opa smiled and placed a hand on my shoulder without moving his eyes from the game in play. The house was silent, Oma long asleep, as we studied the board. I pictured the whole town sleeping soundly while we sat there on the floor. I pushed my mind back to the task at hand, the game.

I ran through all the possible first moves. Then I looked at the most promising, and projected all the possible second moves. Finally, I took the best second moves and thought up all the possible third moves. This was the way Opa had taught me how to play.

Most players only thought one or two moves ahead. The key, he said, was to be one more step ahead. Funny, that was my father's belief about how to run a good con game, too. Keep at least one step ahead of the other guy. My grandfather and I had been playing together almost every night. The game was always accompanied by conversation about more than just the game itself.

It hit me like a bright light suddenly shining in my face. Nd3, check. Mr. Alexandria's only escape would be to c8, and an easy checkmate would follow. I worked it through a second time. Then a third, just to make sure. There was no mistake. Each time it worked perfectly.

"I see it, Opa. You've won . . . you've won!"

"Yes, I believe I have. In a few more weeks, after we have mailed our last moves, I will know for sure. Mr. Alexandria is like an eel the way he can get out of tight places."

"But not this place, Opa. Not this time," I said excitedly.

"I believe you are right, Jonathan." He continued to stare at the chessboard.

"I guess Mr. Alexandria is sound asleep and doesn't even know he's lost, yet," I said.

"No, probably not sleeping, unless he is a very late sleeper." He turned over his wrist and looked at his watch. "Moscow is seven hours later than here, so it is now almost 10:00 in the morning."

He now turned his attention to me. "That was very considerate of you to wake up, leave your warm bed at 3:00 in the morning and come downstairs to help me with my chess game. That is why you are here, is it not?"

"Not exactly. I was having problems sleeping. I've got things on my mind."

"Ah," he said, nodding. "I have had that difficulty myself on many a night. A thought goes round and round and round inside your head. Each time it goes around you think that you will discover the answer, and, each time there is no answer."

It was my turn to nod. I swallowed hard before beginning again. "Opa . . . I know you don't like my father. I heard you talking about him the first night I was here. I know you don't agree with the way he makes his money, the things he does, but he always knows what to say. He knows how to put words together to get people to do what he wants. I just never know what to say."

He took a sip from his mug. "Your father was, is, very good at saying the right words. But there were many things your father did with those words that I do not like. That I even hate."

I knew what he meant. There were times he used words as weapons, to hurt or wound people. Sometimes he aimed those words at me.

"Jonathan, it has never mattered to me very much what a person says. I always listen with my eyes."

I couldn't figure out what he was saying. I shook my head, and he continued his thought. "That means I listen to the words, but more important, I watch what people do after they have spoken the words."

It seemed more clear to me now. "So what you're saying is that you don't trust anybody. You watch them to make sure they don't con you."

An expression I couldn't understand flashed across his face. I thought it was disappointment, but it was gone as quickly as it had appeared and was replaced by his usual look of calm.

"You understand part of it, my grandson. Much more than I understood at your age. It is not that I do not trust people, but rather that I trust everybody."

Now I was completely lost.

"I know this is hard to understand. Maybe I am not explaining it very clearly, Jonathan. You see, I believe that all people are basically good. They know what is right, and what is wrong, and they truly want to do the right thing. They will say words that show they want to do the right thing." He took another sip from his coffee. "But, somewhere between saying the right words and doing the right thing, they are stopped. They are stopped because it is easier to do it a different way, or they get confused, or they think somebody else will do it, or they run away, or . . . they are just too afraid."

He took another long drink from his mug. It had been sitting there a long time and I was sure it was stone cold by now. He saw me watching him drink.

"How rude of me. Would you like a cup of good strong Dutch coffee? I am sure it would help you get to sleep . . ." he paused, " . . . sometime next week." He laughed softly as he pushed himself away from the table and stood up. He offered me his hand and pulled me to my feet. "Jonathan, you have not told me of your problems, but I can tell you the answer."

He walked across the room, opened the door, and turned off the light. The room was dark. The only light now was the tiny trickle still flowing from my room. It formed a path linking my room upstairs, at the far end of the house, with the spot where we stood. His silhouette, but not his face, was all that I could see.

"Jonathan, do the thing you believe is right. The words, if you even need words, will follow."

We walked from the den and followed the trail up the stairs. He took my hand as we walked. At the top of the stairs he gave me a hug and we separated.

Just as I got to the door of my room, he called out to me.

"Jonathan, do you know what is the right thing to do?"

"I know," I answered. I just didn't know if I could do it.

Nineteen

"I'll see you guys tomorrow. I'm catching a ride with my grandfather. We have to go somewhere," I said to Tommy and Stan.

They said good-bye and were soon gone. I shuffled the papers and books in my locker, keeping an eye on Mr. Roberts's classroom door. A few minutes after the last kid came out, I closed up my locker and peeked in the door. Mr. Roberts was sitting there, leaning back in his chair, shoes off, feet on his desk, tie loosened, reading. In the background his CD player cranked out music. I almost broke out laughing when he started singing along in a high falsetto voice. I knocked on the door loudly.

He snapped out of his trance, looking startled and somewhat embarrassed. He took his feet down and tried to straighten his tie.

"Jonathan, what a surprise to see you here. You're usually long gone when that bell rings. If it wasn't for Vern, you'd get the Olympic gold medal in school exiting."

"Yeah, it's a bit of a surprise to me, too."

He reached over and turned down his CD player. "I love listening to Motown. Not your kind of music though, is it?"

"No, not really, although I did enjoy hearing you inging along," I teased.

"Thank you for that compliment," he answered. Now, why are you here?"

"Well, Mr. Roberts, I was hoping to —"

"Make a deal?" he said, completing my sentence.

"Yeah, a deal," I confirmed. "Maybe I shouldn't say anything, but you see, there's this fight supposed to appen —"

He interrupted. "At the water tower, this Friday, after school."

"But . . . how did you know?" I stumbled, feeling confused. I shouldn't have been surprised that he knew. In some ways it was even reassuring.

"For some reason kids assume that all adults, especially teachers, are both stupid and deaf," he stated. Now, go on, Jonathan. I'm listening."

I took a deep breath. "It has to do with belonging."

* * *

By the time Mr. Roberts and I had finished our business, there weren't that many kids left in the halls. I exited out the side door and came around to the front of the school, where I was going to meet my grandfather. It was almost by habit that I still used the side door. Over the last month I'd come to know every side door and service exit in the entire school. Until I'd paid everybody back, and I was most of the way there by now, I'd figured it was better to avoid going out the same door every day. I had paid the loudest and biggest first. Although it burnt me to do it, this meant that Alexander and Justin were the first in line. They still hassled me, but now it was because they just enjoyed being jerks instead of because of any money I owed them. You might say that now they were doing it for pleasure instead of for business.

Opa was leaning against the fender of our truck parked out in front of the school. Usually there was a whole line of fancy cars waiting for students. Almost always the kids being picked up were from the Heights. It struck me as funny that those kids who only had a few blocks to walk often had rides waiting, while us townies, who had so much farther to go, had none. This was the first time Opa had been at school since he dropped me off when I started at Vista. By this time most of the expensive cars had left, leaving the pickup truck with only a few other vehicles for company.

Although I could see my grandfather clearly, he hadn't yet caught sight of me. I stood there, just watching him. I'd been observing him a lot lately. Not the way I'd watched him when I first got here. It was a strange sort of feeling, but it seemed that just looking at him made me feel safer, or calmer, or even a little happier. It may be hard to understand, because it certainly is hard to explain, but just being around him made me feel more solid.

He finally saw me. He gave me a slight smile and made a subtle movement of his head to motion me over. I jogged to the passenger side of the truck. He gestured to the floor of the pickup. There were four flats of flowers. One contained nothing but carnations.

"You got the flowers," I said, nervously stating the obvious.

"Just as we discussed. I think the carnations will be very lovely," he added.

We climbed into the truck. He carefully adjusted his rearview mirror and put on his seatbelt. I put on mine as well as he eased us away from the gravel shoulder and onto the roadway.

We didn't talk much as we drove. That much hadn't changed since our first drive together. Now, though, it was a very comfortable silence. Words weren't always necessary between us. Silence can speak volumes.

The late April rain that had been threatening to fall all day started to pelt down against the window.

"I do not think that the plants will mind the rain too much," he noted. "I brought with me a pair of work overalls for you. Oma would be mad as a wet cat at both of us if you got your school clothing all dirty."

"Thanks," I replied.

"For me, the rain seems correct. It seems wrong to go there when the sun is shining brightly. The rain feels better," he said.

I didn't reply. I just stared through the windshield, at the wipers pulsing away the drops.

"I am glad that you wanted to come with me, Jonathan. Is it still all right? Do you still wish to come?"

I felt a catch in my throat. "I'm not really sure if I do want to come, but it's the right thing to do."

Without taking his eyes off the road, he reached over with one of his massive hands and squeezed my leg.

"I think she'll like the carnations. She always liked carnations." It was one of the few clear memories of her that I had. She liked carnations. That evening when I found my opa leafing through the flower catalogue, I had mentioned it to him.

"I know that you are right, Jonathan. And I like that you are coming with me. Each year the times that I go there, I go alone. This time it will not seem so lonely."

He slowed the truck, and we turned, through the gates and into the cemetery. It was ironic. This was only the second time I'd ever been in a cemetery. Same cemetery, both times with him right beside me.

He drove up the curving lane, away from the church guarding the gate. I looked back through the window. No long line of cars following us this time. The town still could be seen in the distance, but the new subdivisions, the Vista estates, bridged the town and the cemetery.

He pulled the truck over and stopped. He got out of the cab while I struggled to pull the old grey overalls over top of my clothes. Opa got out the four flats of flowers, some work gloves and two shovels. He handed me a pair of the gloves, and I picked up two of the flats. He carried the other two and both shovels.

Wordlessly we wandered up the hill, through the rows of headstones. The rain was falling more strongly now. I absentmindedly read the names and dates engraved in the stones. Some were so worn down by the weather that the writing had been lost. The grounds were well kept. The grass was short, a few trees were bursting into full spring bloom, and a high wall surrounded the grounds. It seemed so much smaller than I remembered it. So much smaller. In my mind I had pictured it going on endlessly.

I could see a fresh grave, covered with flowers, in the distance. But most of the graves were vacant, with no flowers and only a few weeds as markers. People forgot. They had to move on in their lives and didn't have the time to tend a grave.

"Here it is, Jonathan," he said quietly.

It was a simple white stone, about a metre high. In front of the stone was a turned piece of ground, weedless and ready for planting. I looked at the inscription.

Christina Moore (née van Gees)
Beloved daughter of Herbert and Velta
Wife of David Moore
Mother of Jonathan
Your memory lives on in all of us

Opa had already started to work, taking the individual plants from the flats, while the words reverberated in my mind. Your memory lives on in all of us.

He was on his knees, his face partially turned away from me. He'd stopped working and was just looking off into space. His expression looked peaceful. He wasn't moving.

"Opa, are you all right?" I finally asked.

"I am okay. I was just thinking. Thinking about your mother. She was such a gentle soul. You do not know how many times she would bring home a stray dog or cat. She could not think of them being alone or cold or hungry. The same with people. She could never stand to see somebody in pain. She always wanted to help." He paused and then turned to face me. "Sometimes, I have forgotten things I should have remembered. In trying to forget about the pain, I forgot about all the good things. Having you here these last few months has helped me to remember the good."

"I only wish I could remember more. Sometimes I don't think I even remember enough to miss her," I answered. "I wish I could have known her a little longer."

Opa got up off the ground, his pants stained from the mud. He reached an arm around me, and I felt his body shelter me from the rain.

"Nothing can change what has happened, Jonathan. But, God willing, we can help what comes next."

Twenty

"That was a good meal, Velta. I must excuse myself. I have a few errands to run around town," Opa said as he rose from the dining room table.

"Oh, that would be fine," started Oma. I kicked her under the table. "I mean, NO!" she practically shouted. "I cooked the dinner, Jonathan set the table and you did nothing but sit here and eat. Now you want us to clean up, too!"

She stood up and marched around the table. Reaching up, she grabbed Opa by the ear. He was stunned and his mouth dropped open.

"Close your mouth and come with me to the kitchen right now. You may be big but not too big to help with the dishes! Do not get me any madder," she threatened.

She winked at me out of the corner of her eye as she pulled him out of the room. He followed behind her, without protest, and I visualized him being one of those gigantic hot air balloons being towed along in a parade.

I looked at my watch. It was 4:55. Five more minutes to go. I stacked the plates and carried them into the kitchen. I pushed open the swinging door with my backside and entered the kitchen in time to catch my opa's apology, mid-sentence.

" . . . honestly I am sorry. I did not mean to upset ou so. I do not even remember when you have been his mad at me. I will try to help more with the ishes . . ." he pleaded.

The rest of the sentence was cut off as I went back nto the dining room for another load and the door wung shut behind me. Grabbing a few more plates, I ushed back in to hear his continued pleas.

" . . . why do you not sit down, dear? I will finish the lishes all by myself."

I tried not to laugh as I glanced at my watch — :59 — one more minute.

"RI-I-ING," the phone sang out.

"Just you keep working, Herbert. I will get that hone," she said as she moved across the kitchen and icked up the receiver. "Hello . . . yes, yes, of course 'll accept the charges. Hello. I am most pleased to talk o you."

I watched Opa trying to wash the dishes without naking any noise so he could hear what Oma was aying. He had no idea who was on the phone. I knew.

"Yes," she said into the phone, "he is right here. He as a few things to clean up before he can come to the hone." She glanced over at him and silently mouthed he words "keep working" with a threatening look on ier face.

"While we are waiting for him, please tell me what s the weather like? Uh huh, uh huh . . . yes . . . ah, very imilar to here. I think he is now finished. I will get iim. And thank you for calling." She put the phone lown. "Herbert, there is a gentleman on the phone 'or you. You can finish your dishes later. Can you take he phone . . . in the den."

He had already dried off his hands and was walking across the kitchen when her last words spun him

around and aimed him for the den. Oma broke int
laughter as he left the room, her hand over the mouth
piece of the phone.

"And, Jonathan, you come and take this extension.

I dropped the dishes I was carrying into the sink
She passed me the phone in time for me to hear Op
pick up the line.

"Hello. This is Herbert van Gees."

"Good evening, Herbert van Gees. This is Bori
Sergi Alexandria."

There was a definite pause on my opa's part. "Mr
Alexandria, I am both surprised and pleased to receiv
this call. To what do I owe such a pleasure?"

"Ah, it is definitely a pleasure, and we both owe thi
long overdue conversation to your Jonathan," said Mr
Alexandria.

"Jonathan! But how?"

I entered into the conversation. "I'm here, Opa, or
the other line."

"Hello, Jonathan. This is Boris. It is good to hear
your voice again."

"Hello, Mr. Alexandria. Thanks for calling," I re
plied.

"You are most welcome, Jonathan. Herbert?"

"Yes, Mr. Alexandria?" he answered.

"Herbert, after these seventeen long years we have
been friends, do you not think you could call me
Boris?"

"Da, da, of course I can, Boris. Now, could someone
please explain things to me," asked Opa.

"Of course," Boris's voice crackled over the phone
"Three days ago I was called by your Jonathan."

"Oma helped me make the call," I interjected.

"Jonathan asked me if I would consider finishing

our game by telephone rather than by mail. He generously offered to pay for the call," Boris said.

"Out of my savings," I added.

"He said it was his birthday present for you. Happy birthday, Herbert," Boris said.

"Thank you."

"Naturally, I could not turn down such a thoughtful and generous offer. After he called, I turned my attention to the game in progress. I understood his excitement," Boris continued.

"Shall we proceed with the game then?" Opa enquired.

"Da, da, we should proceed. But I fear it is not a game as much as merely my execution."

"I wish you no ill will, Boris, but I hope it will be, as you say, an execution."

"And for the sake of Jonathan's savings, we should hope for a quick execution," added Boris.

"Jonathan, come and join me in the den. I would enjoy your company."

"Yes, Opa, and thanks and good-bye, Mr. Alexandria."

I hung up the phone and sped out of the kitchen. The door swung shut, cutting off Oma's yell, "Jonathan, do not run in . . ."

* * *

I sat by his side as he won the game. They talked about meeting, next year, while Mr. Alexandria was on a tour of North America.

Opa smiled during the delayed celebration dessert Oma had prepared as a surprise. He smiled when we went for a walk together, the three of us, that evening.

He smiled when he put me to bed. And he probably smiled all through his sleep that night.

But I was even happier than him.

Twenty-one

Dear Dad,

I know it's been a while since I wrote. I hope you got my other letters and get this one, too.

I've been here even longer than we were in Tupper Lake. I'm only nine weeks from finishing the school year here.

My room is really neat. Opa and I made a great bed for me. Actually, he did most of the work, but I helped. I've had it for a long time now. You should see it! I also put up all my old posters. At first, Oma didn't want me to because she said the tacks would leave holes in the walls. Then she said it didn't matter because I'd already filled more important holes. Before, I wouldn't have known what she meant by that. Now I understand. I guess I'm just getting older.

I've been saving my money. I have over two hundred dollars. I have a job working at Opa's old company. It's called Bear Woodworking. Did you know that my mother designed the sign?

I work there some days after school and every Saturday morning. Mostly I just clean up and move things. Sometimes they let me actually build things. You don't have to worry because everybody watches over me to make sure I'm safe. It's like having thirty parents. So far I've built a neat lamp, a bookshelf and a table. The table leans a bit to one side, but I think I can fix it. Everybody says I have a way with wood. All the men in the shop are friendly and nice to me. At first I figured it was because they like Opa but now I know they treat me that way because they like me.

School is going okay. Mr. Roberts is the toughest teacher I ever had. He doesn't let anybody get away with anything. He's been spending extra time with me and my best friend Tommy to help us with our math. I'm really not that bad anymore. There are still some kids at my school I don't like or get along with. But I have some good friends, too. Besides Tommy, there is also Vern and Stan.

I know that you have been really busy making money to come and get me. It's okay if it takes you a little longer.

Your son,

Jonathan

Twenty-two

By the time I had picked up the things I needed, Tommy had already got off school property. He had reached the path that led through the forest to the water tower.

"Hey, wait up!" I yelled. Tommy turned around and stopped. When I caught up, I was startled to see that he was wearing a team sweater with "Streetsville" written across the front. It had number ninety-nine on the back, blue on blue, and it was well-worn, with rips repaired in more than one place.

"Mind if I walk with you?" I asked.

"I'm not going home," he replied.

"Gee, thanks for the information. I thought you'd moved out of town and were living in the forest."

"You know what I mean. I'm headed for the tower."

"I know you're not going home. I know you're heading for the tower. What I want to know is if I can walk with you?"

"Part way, or all the way?" he asked.

"All the way . . . if you'll let me."

His expression didn't change as he answered. "I'd be right happy if you did."

We started walking. He was moving at a fast pace, and I kept in lock step. The path was a narrow slit of dirt cut between towering trees. At times it wasn't wide enough for us both to pass side by side, and I would fall back to follow behind. There was a steady incline to the path and regular outcroppings of rocks that we needed to scale. The tower was located on the highest spot in the area to allow gravity to feed the water down to the town.

As we continued our pace, in silence, I could feel my heart beating faster and my breath becoming more laboured.

"You must be starting to feel a little tight," Tommy stated.

I nodded.

"It's the same feeling I used to get before a big game. Excited and anxious," Tommy said.

When he said that, I knew I had found my opening, my chance to start things rolling in the direction I wanted them to move. One of the first rules of chess and con games is to look for the right opening.

"Do you miss it, Tommy, the sports?"

"Yeah, I miss it something awful. I love playing sports. I loved putting on this sweater and playing. There's nothing better than fighting for something, trying as hard as you can. Some people think it has to do with winning, but for me, that isn't what it's all about. I'd rather play my best and lose than get an easy win. It isn't about winning, it's about trying."

As Tommy was talking, I had the strangest sensation. I was seeing his mouth move, and I was hearing his voice, but it was like my opa was talking.

"It's real sad you don't get to play anymore. It's a shame you don't get to play for Vista . . ." I paused. "Like I do."

"What?" he said, stopping to turn and face me.

As he did so, I undid my jacket and slipped it off to reveal that I was wearing a blue and gold Vista Heights

Public School sweater. I could see the muscles in his neck strain and bulge. His face took on a look of confusion and then hurt. When he spoke, he spoke quietly.

"What are you doing in that sweater? Are you one of them?"

I had expected him to be angry, maybe even to take a swing at me. What I wasn't ready for was how hurt he looked. I had never seen him look so fragile before. I had never seen him look beat.

"You know, Tommy, sometimes you can be real stupid. I didn't come up here to fight for Streetsville Public School. It's just an empty building to me. I don't want to fight anybody. I'm just tired of them telling me that Vista isn't my school, that I'm not good enough to belong there. That school belongs to me, and to you, just as much as it belongs to them. I'm here because nobody can take away where I belong. And besides, you're my friend, and friends have got to stick together."

Tommy nodded. I could see him thinking. As my opa would say, "I could almost smell the wood burning." I thought it was the right time to go for the whole ball of wax.

"There's one more thing, Tommy," I said as I pulled another Vista team sweater out of my bag. "I want you to put this on."

His response was instant and angry, more of what I'd expected. "I'm not taking off my Streetsville sweater!" he said defiantly.

"Nobody's asking you to take off your old sweater, just like nobody's asking you to forget about where you come from. Put it on over top. We're all like onions, we keep on growing and adding layers, but that doesn't mean we lose what we already have inside of us. That's what my opa told me."

Again, I knew he was thinking. He leaned against a tree and then sat down at its base. I slid down beside him. We sat in silence, the only sound coming from the birds that fluttered about through the surrounding trees.

My father always said that this time, when people were thinking, was the time to move in for the "kill." When a person is battling to find the right answer, while they're still undecided, you slide in and push them in the direction you want them to go. I wasn't here to push Tommy, or to con him, or scam him, or trick him, or get something out of him. I was here to help him, and to help myself, too. He needed time, and silence, to make up his own mind.

I watched as he slowly took the sweater from my hands. He held it and felt the material. His fingers ran around the outline of the crest and lettering. It was as if he were seeing one of these sweaters for the first time. In a way, he was. This was the first time he was being asked to see the possibility of one of these sweaters being on his back.

"This doesn't mean I've forgotten about Streetsville," he said as he began to slip the jersey over his head. "It just means that maybe I think you're right about some things."

We continued our walk up the incline of the hill, following the path as it weaved through the trees and bumped over rocks. Tommy explained that it was important for us to get there first and have a chance to rest before they got there.

Tommy told me that the old water tower wasn't used anymore. Since the new water system had been developed, the tower had outlived its purpose. It just sat up there on the hill, part way full of water, too big and expensive to take down. Just like the old town and the old school, this tower stood for something in Tommy's mind, and I knew without asking that he had chosen this as the site of the fight. Nobody ever came up there except for the occasional couple looking for privacy or teenagers looking for trouble. Guaranteed, this was a place where we wouldn't be disturbed. Or rescued.

When we got within fifty metres of the tower, Tommy picked up a rock and hurled it at the base. It made a metallic ring. As we continued to move closer we both picked up rocks and hurled them at the tower. Different sized rocks made different sounds when they hit the metal. Some sounded dull, others sharp, and some reminded me of the first note played by a calypso steel drum band.

Tossing the rocks, I felt carefree and forgot why we were headed to the tower. Now, as we finally reached it, I remembered exactly why we were here. My legs felt a little shaky, and I needed to sit down. Almost as if he could read my mind, Tommy took a seat at the base of the tower, his back against it.

The coolness of the water in the tower passed through the metal, through my sweater, and right into my back. It sent a shiver running along my spine. I wasn't sure if we were sitting there to get out of the sun or so nobody could come up behind us. Maybe for both reasons.

The old tower stood over thirty metres tall. It was painted green and white, and the colours were still amazingly bright despite the small patches of rust that bled through like freckles.

"What are the rules of this fight?" I asked.

"Rules?"

"Yeah, what are the rules?"

"It's pretty simple, really. They'll try to hit us and

hurt us and we'll try to hit them and hurt them. You think you can follow that?"

I think I understood pretty good. We sat and waited. In the distance, at first so quiet that I hoped I was just imagining it, I heard the sound of people. People moving toward us. The noise got louder and louder. It sounded like there were a lot of them coming. I turned to Tommy. His eyes were closed. I was thinking how brave he was to just sit there and wait so peacefully. I didn't feel brave.

"Tommy . . . I know this may sound stupid . . . but I'm scared."

"I think you'd be stupid if you weren't. I'm afraid, too."

"You're scared?" His answer had caught me completely off guard.

He opened his eyes and looked at me. "Whenever I have to do something like this I'm scared. Each time, part of me wants to just get up and run. Everybody wants to turn tail and run, sometimes." He paused, as if he was thinking through what he just said. He probably had thought these thoughts many times before but had never spoken them to anybody. "It's not too late, Jonathan. If you want to leave, I'll understand."

"It's not too late for you either . . . but I think we're going to stay."

Tommy gave me a slight smile and reached over and patted me on the leg.

Almost as if on cue we heard voices, loud voices, coming from the woods. Seconds later they broke through the forest cover into the clearing surrounding the tower. There were nine, no, ten of them. Some of the kids I had expected to be here, people like Alexander, Justin, and Shaun. They were leading the way. Behind them came Daniel, Nick, and Brian. They were from the Heights but always acted okay. Then, there were some others I didn't know by name.

They came out of the underbrush, singing the Vista school song. When the gang saw us, almost all at once, they stopped singing. I think they were surprised to see two of us waiting, but much more shocked when they realized that we were wearing Vista Heights team sweaters.

We stood up, and they continued to walk toward us until we stood face-to-face, only an arm's length apart. I'd never felt this scared before. And there was nobody, not even my father, to rescue me this time. I hoped no one could see that my legs were shaking. Heck, I wished nobody could see any part of me. I wanted to believe that if I stood perfectly still they might, somehow, not even see me. I prayed for invisibility. As I caught Justin staring me squarely in the face, I quickly realized that I had not vanished from view.

"What are you two townies doing wearing those sweaters?" Alexander snarled.

The rest of the crew mumbled similar sentiments. Tommy just smiled sweetly. I knew he was enjoying catching them off guard like this. It was a minor victory, but judging from the unequal numbers, probably the only one we'd see this afternoon.

Justin spoke directly to me. "You must be awfully dumb to come up here, really dumb!"

I tried to answer, but once again no words seemed to come. My mouth was dry and my tongue rubbery.

Tommy slapped me on the back. "You know, Jonathan, he might be right. Maybe you are dumb. After all, when it comes to dumb, Justin here is an expert. I've never met anybody in my whole life who knows more about being dumb than Justin."

In spite of it all, I found myself laughing out loud. Looking past the front four of our opposition, I saw that a few of them were quietly snickering and chuckling at Tommy's words, too.

"Forget about that. Where did you guys get those sweaters?" Alexander spoke with such force that little bits of spit flew out of his mouth.

Tommy again smiled sweetly. "I guess we should tell them, shouldn't we, Jonathan?"

I nodded, relieved that I'd get a chance to explain things while I still had all the teeth I'd need to articulate all the words.

"Let me tell them," Tommy added.

Again I nodded, forgetting that Tommy didn't have a clue how we got those sweaters. Before I could interrupt, he started talking again.

"A little while before you, ah, gentlemen arrived, we found two lost lambs from Vista. It didn't surprise us to find people from Vista who were lost, so, wanting to be helpful, we told them where to go. I'm even willing to tell all of you where to go. Anyway, they left their sweaters in gratitutde for our help."

The story was obviously a joke, but nobody was laughing. I could see the ten of them starting to come together, like a gang. Kids can be just like farm dogs. Alone they can be friendly, play with you, lick your hand, but put a bunch of them together and they go out and kill sheep. They were starting to look like a pack of dogs, and I was starting to feel like mutton.

I swallowed hard and worked up some spit to help lubricate my words. Finally the words were able to slide out.

"Mr. Roberts gave us these sweaters. Doesn't everybody on the Vista Heights soccer team get sweaters?"

Everyone froze, like we were playing statue or something.

"Yeah, Tommy's the starting inside centre, and I'll probably be playing, um, midfield, or maybe defence."

The silence was deafening. Tommy looked even more confused than the others. He had a look on his face like his mind had been working so hard to make sense of all this that it had overheated, melted, and fused into a giant clump of pinky-grey Jell-O.

Alexander broke the silence. He was somebody who could be at a loss for thought but never for words. "You two are on the Vista Heights soccer team?"

I didn't know whether he meant this as a question, or a statement, or if he was just saying the words one more time to see if it made any more sense coming from his own lips.

"You heard me. We're on the Vista soccer team." By the third time I figured even Alexander would understand. "And, I guess that makes us all teammates. We're all on the same side."

Almost instantly the gang dissolved into little subgroups. The kids I only knew by sight, sensing there wasn't going to be any fight, immediately drifted away from the tower and started back down the trail that would lead back to the school. They vanished into the brush.

Brian, Dan, and Nick came up to us and, all excited, started to ask questions. They were all on the soccer team. Tommy was nothing short of a local legend. Having him play on the team meant a chance for them all to share in the glory of a championship season. Tommy's brain had unfused enough that he was able to smile one of his grins and nod occasionally. We all agreed to meet at school early Monday morning for a little extra practice before the real one started that morning. They were thrilled, and their goodbyes were warm and friendly as they started back down to the school.

Tommy slapped me on the back. "That was beautiful! We won and we didn't even have to fight anybody. Of course, not fighting can be a bit disappointing."

I nodded weakly. I was watching the four remaining kids out of the corner of my eye. Alexander was leading an animated conversation, just out of earshot. I could hear their voices but couldn't quite make out the words. All at once Justin's voice rose, and I could understand what he was saying.

"I don't care if they are on the team. We came up here to beat the stuffing out of somebody, and I'm not leaving until somebody has had the stuffing beaten out of them!"

I turned to Tommy. "I don't think you're going to be disappointed."

Justin and Alexander, followed by the other two, came menacingly in our direction.

"Stop!" I yelled as they advanced to within an arm's length of us. "Before we get started, I have something I want to say. This fight's got nothing to do with the old school. Vista belongs to me and Tommy as much as it belongs to you four jerks. We're as good as you, and you can't chase us away. But, even though you're all jerks, there is one thing Justin said that's true. Somebody's gonna get the stuffing beaten out of them before you leave."

The last distinct memory I have is of my fist meeting Alexander's face. I thought I might like it better than the other way. What followed was fuzzy as the six of us went at it.

I don't really know if you can say we won or we lost,

but we did try. And like Tommy said, trying is the important part.

* * *

The walk back from the tower didn't seem nearly as long as the walk there — partly because it was all downhill but mostly because of the things we left behind. These included not only our four classmates, who needed time to "rest" before starting down, but also things like anger and fear and uncertainty. Things like that can really weigh you down.

We moved along at a good clip, jumping off the rocks and leaping up to touch overhanging tree branches.

"Jonathan, how did you ever come up with that story about the sweaters?" Tommy asked, shaking his head in disbelief.

"What do you mean, story? Almost everything I told them is true."

"Come on. You're kidding me now, too."

"Nope. I got the sweaters from Mr. Roberts. We're on the soccer team. You'll be starting for the team when we play next Wednesday."

"I thought you were just making the whole thing up. You mean I'm really on the team, the *Vista Heights* team?"

"That's right. You are going to play, aren't you?" I asked apprehensively.

"Well, I guess I will. I mean, I wouldn't want to let my new teammates down."

"Good. If you didn't play, especially after we got these sweaters all dirty, I think I'd have to fight Mr. Roberts come Monday morning."

We continued to walk while the reality of the situation sank in for Tommy. "What part isn't true?" he finally asked.

"Well, I am going to be on the team, too, but I don't think that there's much chance of me starting. When I asked Mr. Roberts if I could, he mentioned something about if the whole team caught chicken pox, there was a slight chance I could be in the starting lineup."

Tommy chuckled. "That's just like Roberts. He knows a good soccer player when he sees one, or when he doesn't see one."

"Hey, don't rub it in. I may not be a great soccer player, but you're lucky I'm not a bad fighter. I saved your bacon today."

"Jonathan, I got some news for you. Compared with how you fight, you are one truly great soccer player." He playfully cuffed me on the side of the head. "One more thing, Jonathan."

"Yeah?"

"Thanks."

Twenty-three

"You should not be getting into fights, young man," Oma was saying. "We are not raising you to be a prizefighter. And hold still. I have to make sure we get all the dirt out of these cuts and scrapes."

"Ow, that hurts," I yelled.

"Good. I am glad it hurts! Now sit still or I will have your opa sit on top of you. Herbert, I want you to talk to your grandson."

Without acknowledging her request, he rose from his chair at the far end of the kitchen. He had been watching everything in silence, letting Oma do all the talking. He headed for the back door and motioned with his hand for me to follow. I got up and followed.

He crossed the backyard, heading to his workshop. He unlocked the door, and we walked into the darkness. Then he flicked on the switch, and the room was bathed in light. The lathes, the drills and drill press, the sanders and big circular saw with its ominous finger-eating teeth were all still and silent. Despite all the time I'd spent around these machines, the circular saw still made me nervous. I instinctively tried to put my hands in my pockets, but my right one was becoming even more swollen and painful to the touch.

"Sit down, Jonathan."

"Yes, sir." It sounded so natural now to call him that. As natural as it was to call him Opa.

We sat there, silently. The seconds stretched into minutes. I could see him searching, searching for the right words. Finally, he spoke.

"Your mother and I . . . would have talks here . . . not really talks . . . I would talk . . . sometimes I would yell . . . and she would listen, or I hoped she would listen." He spoke so quietly now I had to lean forward to hear him. He was looking into the distance like he was watching something.

"The last time she and I talked . . . or I talked, she just listened . . . I told her she was making a big mistake. I warned her about your father. I told her she had to choose. I told her that if she left my home, if she closed that door, it would never open again." He paused again. His face looked strained and distorted with emotion as he struggled to find words. "When she left, I prayed and hoped I would see my daughter . . . my baby, again. I did not see her for eight long years, not until the day we buried her. I always thought there would be time, but time ran out. I loved your mother more than I have ever loved anything in this life. I never stopped loving her, but I could not tell her. I was so proud and so strong, but I was not strong enough to open up the door again." He leaned forward, paused, looked at me, and took my hand in his.

"Now, Jonathan, you are here, and I see your mother . . . your oma, and even a little bit of me, and maybe even some good parts from your father. This is your home, Jonathan. That door will never be closed to you. I want you to know . . . to know how much I love you."

Through the tears in my eyes I could see the tears

coming from his. I crossed the space that separated us, and he held me so gently, so softly in his arms. No words were spoken. No words were needed.

Time passed. I remained within the safety of Opa's arms.

"Jonathan, Oma says that I am to talk to you."

"Yes, sir."

"Who were you fighting with?"

"I don't think you'd know them. They go to my school, but they live up on the hill."

"You were fighting more than one boy?"

"Tommy and I."

"Tommy Kraemer?"

"Yes, sir."

"Tommy is a good boy. I know his family. I worked with his grandfather. If he is anything like his grandfather, he would not start a fight, but he could certainly finish one. Did you boys start the fight?"

"Not really."

"Did you fight for a good reason?"

"Yes, sir."

"Will you have to fight again?"

I thought about this question. "Probably, but . . . maybe not."

"Well, I hope not as well, but if you have to, you better eat more of Oma's dumplings. We need to put more meat on your bones. Come now, we should go in."

I climbed off his lap but didn't let go of his hand. We moved together to the door, and he switched off the light. It was very dark as we walked across the yard.

"Now, remember. When we get back inside, tell Oma that I gave you a good talking to. Try to look like I scared you a little, and try not to look so proud."

I realized I was feeling proud. It wasn't about the

fighting, but about not running, about the things that Opa said, about the look in his eyes when we talked.

* * *

Lying in bed later that night, my hand throbbed with pain. No aspirin. Oma had said she wasn't going to help ease the pain, because any silly fool who got himself hurt like this deserved to feel a little pain ("maybe it will make you think twice the next time").

I had one more thing to do. I set the alarm to wake me up in an hour. By then my grandparents would be asleep. I took the alarm clock and put it under my pillow. That way when it went off it would wake me but wouldn't rouse them.

My tongue ran over the inside of my mouth. I could feel a few small cuts and still detect the taste of my blood. The bed felt good. The sheets were cool and clean and soft. There was a gentle breeze blowing in through the window. I felt a warm glow start to radiate from the back of my head, down my body, all the way into my feet. I was thinking about the surprise birthday party that Stacy told me she was giving for Jennifer in a few weeks. I wondered what I was going to wear. I felt at peace. I closed my eyes and drifted off to sleep.

* * *

The gentle buzz of the alarm percolated up through the pillow. I reached underneath, and for an instant, the alarm became louder. I shut it off and listened. There wasn't a sound. It hadn't disturbed anybody else.

Noiselessly I swung my feet from the bed onto the floor. The upstairs was completely dark, and I quietly moved into the hall. Stopping at the top of the stairs, I glanced at my grandparents' door. It was closed, no light showing under the crack, and there were no sounds. I went down the steps. All twelve of them. I had mapped the whole house thoroughly and had, months before, practised moving through the darkness, just like at that foster home, readying myself for the escape.

The living room curtains were parted, and a film of silvery light cast by a streetlight flowed in and shone off the surfaces of the furniture, giving the room an eerie feeling. In the middle stood the green chair. I pushed my shoulder against it and it slid away. The sound of the legs grating against the floor seemed loud against the silence of the house, and it sent a shiver up my spine. I stopped and listened. Nothing. No sound. Without moving, I looked up at the stairs. I saw only darkness.

I sank to my knees and started to feel for the seams. It was at that point that I had the ominous feeling I wasn't alone. Not a sound as much as a presence. I looked up to see Opa standing in the doorway. He must have fallen asleep on the couch in the den.

Freezing, I held my breath and prayed. Prayed that somehow in the darkness I was hidden and he simply hadn't seen me, motionless in the shadows on the floor.

"Go ahead," he said softly. "If it is the money you are after, go ahead."

I remained silent.

"Go ahead, take the money. It means nothing. You have already taken something more important, something much more important than money." His voice was still deadly quiet.

"I wasn't taking anything. I was . . ."

"Stop!" he ordered. "Stop! It is enough that you are a thief, do not also make me stand here while you lie to me."

"But let me explain," I pleaded.

"No explaining. No reasons. No buts. No deals. You are a liar and a thief, just like your father. And me . . . me . . . I am an old fool."

His voice trailed off and he moved across the floor until he stood towering right over top of me. He placed a hand on the side of the chair and pushed against it with such power it skidded across the floor and smashed into the wall on the far side of the room.

"There. It is no longer in your way. I am going to bed." His voice was shaky and seemed distant, somehow. Then he turned and left the room.

Still kneeling, I heard the sound of his bedroom door open and close, followed by the noise of the bed springs straining under his weight. I stayed on the floor, struggling to make sense, to find an answer, a way out, a solution. I still clutched the bills, two one hundred-dollar bills, tightly in my hand.

There seemed no point in trying to put them back now. I got to my feet and walked to the stairs. I had to tell him. I had to explain. I wasn't *taking* the money. I was trying to put it back, trying to make everything right. I wasn't a thief . . .

Who was I kidding? I was a thief. The proof was right there in my clenched fist. Maybe I had been trying to put the money back, but I was still a thief. "Just like your father," his words echoed in my head. "Just like your father."

I stumbled back up to my room. I wanted to sleep, to pretend this was just a terrible nightmare and that it would be better in the morning. I moved to the bed, my hand touching one of the posts. It felt like even my touch would taint the things we'd done together. "Just like your father." I walked to the window and stared out into the night.

My heart jumped! The inside light in a car down the street turned on for just an instant. Was it the signal? Was it my father? I waited. Almost a minute passed by. If it was him, it would flash again. A short burst of light fled from the car. It was him. My father had come to get me.

Automatically I pulled on my jeans and the shirt lying beside my bed. Oma was always nagging me to hang up my clothes instead of leaving them in a heap on the floor. I went to my drawer and dug into the socks. I pulled out an old red work sock, where I had hidden the rest of my money. Forty-eight dollars, held together by an elastic band. I pulled the bills free. I peeled off two twenties and placed them, along with the two hundred-dollar bills, on top of the dresser. That would pay them back and cover the cost of the long-distance telephone call for Opa's birthday. On the top of the dresser was a picture of the three of us, taken that night, that special night, he had won his game.

Carefully I removed the picture from its plastic frame and slipped it into my pocket. Then I silently moved through the hall and down the stairs one more time. There, by the back door, my sneakers were waiting in their usual place, shoelaces neatly tucked inside.

I unlocked the door and slipped out. The rush of cool night air felt good as it filled my lungs. I sneaked around the side of the house and up the front walk. The gate creaked noisily, and my thoughts raced back to that cold December night when I first arrived. I looked up the street and saw his car parked part way down the block. It wasn't the same one he had when he left me here, but I knew it was his. In this neighbourhood of pickup trucks, station wagons, and family cars, a fast, foreign car stood out like it was from another planet.

The flare of a match, replaced by the soft red glow of a cigarette, became visible through the windshield I walked toward the car. Seconds later I opened the door and swung into the passenger seat.

"How ya doing, Dad?" The words came with great effort. It was my lip that was cut and swollen, but it was my tongue, once again, that felt thick and numb. It was so long since we had last spoken.

"I've been doing really well, Jonnie. Can't you tell by my new wheels? This car cost me a fortune. How have they been treating you?" His words were so smooth and effortless. They flowed with his confidence.

"I'm okay. They've been treating me okay."

"This is a real sense of déjà vu for your old man. It was almost fourteen years ago that I sat here and waited for your mother, the night she ran away with me. She was still foggy in her mind that night and needed some convincing. You know me, I can talk anybody into anything."

I didn't answer. What could I say? He quickly broke the silence. He never did like silence.

"It took me a little longer than I thought it would, kid. Most people are pretty stupid, but sometimes it takes more time to separate them from their money. It must have been torture for you to be here this long. Has that old Dutchman been giving you any troubles?"

"No, everything has been okay."

"I didn't think you'd have any problems with him. He may be big, but he's none too bright. In a battle of wits between him and you, I knew you'd be able to handle him. After all, you've spent years training with a master."

"Everything was okay. He didn't cause me any troubles. Did you get my last letter?"

"Letter? What letter?"

"I sent one just a few days ago, to our drop box."

"No, I didn't get it. Maybe we can pick it up later. I haven't been to that box since before I dropped you off. Funny, I was down that way a couple of times, and thought you might send me a letter, but I just got too busy."

I realized then that he hadn't got any of my letters.

"Anyway, now that I'm here, face-to-face, I don't need to read any letter to know how you're doing. Let me have a better look at you." He turned on the inside light of the car. "Cripes, have you ever grown! It's only been four months, but you look a couple of years older. I guess we'll have to give up those 'cute little boy' scams. Well, enough talking. We better get moving."

He turned off the inside light. I closed my eyes and waited for him to start the engine, for us to start moving away. He didn't move. We sat there in silence. I wondered what he was waiting for? Why weren't we going? I looked over at him. In the very dim glow thrown by the streetlight, I could see that old familiar look on his face. He had an idea, a con. He was just getting ready to set the hook.

"You could go back inside and get your things, but I know that old cheapskate of a grandfather of yours. He probably didn't buy you anything worth taking. Am I right? No stereo or TV or anything like that."

"I have everything I need right here," I answered.

"You know, it isn't that he doesn't have the money.

He has money. He never spends a dime and he never did trust banks. His money is probably in an old sock under his bed."

"No, not in a sock." I said the words so quietly it felt more like I had thought them instead of saying them.

"It sounds like you know where he keeps his money. You know, don't you? You know! Like father, like son. I knew you'd come through for us. I knew you wouldn't always be a liability." He spoke with such excitement, such pride, like I had won a prize or done something wonderful.

"I know where the money is. I know exactly where it is," I said even more quietly.

"But, could you get it? Could you get it, right now, without anybody knowing?"

"I could get it. Right now."

There was a slight pause. I knew he was thinking. Thinking of the right words to say.

"You know, Jonnie, all these years they never once sent you a birthday present. I didn't get any wedding present. I bet they even owed your mother some money when she left." Another slight pause. "They owe you that money, Jonnie. They owe your mother that money. They owe us that money. She'd be proud of you for being able to take back what was hers."

He sounded so convincing, so genuine. With each word he built up more momentum. He had already convinced himself and knew he could convince me, that all he had to do was just find the right words. What choice did I have?

"Jonnie, with that money we can finally get ourselves a home, a home for the two of us. Don't you think your mother would like that, her two men living together in a house."

I nodded. I knew what needed to be done.

I opened the car door and climbed out.

"Jonnie," he called.

I bent down and looked back inside the car.

"Jonnie, you'll do okay. Remember, you're just like your father," he said, flashing me a big smile.

I stared at my father. With the car door open the inside light was on. In the dull glow I could see the expensive material of his clothes. There was a bit of ash on his pants that had floated down from his cigarette. His hair, greying, was neat and stylish as always. His hands, one on the wheel of the car, the other resting on his lap, were soft, with perfectly manicured nails. They were hands that had never worked, or struggled, or built, or created. Then I looked at his eyes, and I could see doubt. In his eyes, I could see that he knew I was looking at him. Maybe seeing him for the first time.

"Jonnie . . . what's wrong? Go and get the money. Come on. It's time for you to come home." His voice was uncertain, shifting, almost shaky. He was struggling for the words, the words that would make me do what he wanted.

"Don't worry, Dad. I do love you and you'll always be my father, but . . . I'm already home."

I walked back to the house and didn't look back. I heard the engine start, roar to life, spray a path of gravel, and then the sound quickly faded into the night.

The house was still dark and quiet as I entered. I took off my shoes, tucked the laces inside, and placed them neatly by the back door, in their place.

Tomorrow I'd try to make things right. I knew it wouldn't be easy. Maybe it wouldn't even be possible. But I had to try.

I took a deep breath. The house smelled clean — Dutch clean — and of freshly baked cookies and lov and caring.

And it was home. A place to stand my ground.